1

*M*onday, January 19, 1987

Inside the San Diego Airport control tower, a thin man in his forties with long arms and tired eyes immersed himself in his stressful job as an air traffic approach controller. He focused on his radar screen, where a graphic display of inbound flights lit up, the rapid dialog from the tower echoing in the background. The pace was frantic, matching the controller's relentless scrutiny of the screen.

"United 327, Lindbergh Approach turn two one zero," he rattled off. Descend and maintain 15,000. Report airport in sight. Contact tower on 118.3. Good day. American 460, traffic eleven o'clock three miles DC3 heading zero seven zero climbing out of five. Delta inbound with information Romeo say again."

He chewed on the end of a pencil, not breaking his gaze

from the radar screen, his eyes occasionally darting to a pair of binoculars.

Meanwhile, jets with landing lights on traced lines of smoke in the afternoon haze over the city as they descended steadily. Voices of inbound pilots crackled over the airwaves, coordinating their descent and approach.

"Lindbergh Approach, Delta two one eight with you at three-five on the profile," one pilot said.

"United 327 down to five," another chimed in, "We have the airport in sight."

A third pilot joined the conversation, "Looking for traffic. Can we level at 7,000 let that DC3 pass below us? 460."

The controller refocused on the screens, adjusting his headset as another voice rang out.

"Lindbergh Approach, this is Japan Airlines flight 719 thirty miles east of the airport inbound with information Sierra."

The air was thick with contention in a meeting room filled with mostly male pilots. From the head of the table, Imani Safe, a bright and assertive executive in her early forties, held her ground. She was a well-dressed professional who exuded a commanding presence. As the National Transportation Safety Board Chairman, she was accustomed to this. Still, the edge in her voice betrayed her relative newness to the role.

"There are two things the Administration wants to accomplish over the next few years," Imani began. One is to upgrade the computer systems at high-density airports, and two is to introduce Airport Radar Service Areas where they're needed."

One seasoned pilot interjected, "A few years back, the FAA

CRASH SITE

A.C. JETT

Questions/comments? The author can be contacted at AuthorACJett@gmail.com.

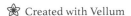 Created with Vellum

director told us this would be an open field where anyone could land."

Imani responded calmly, "You still can."

"But only so long as you're IFR, you got an encoder, a transponder, and a rich uncle to pay for it," he retorted.

Lester Stone, the FAA Western Director, interceded. He was a timid-looking bureaucrat in his mid-fifties whose voice had seen better days. He was clearly battling the flu. "I think we can let the Chairman explain," he rasped.

"When we put the Terminal Radar Service Areas into effect, it was to make flying safer for everyone, not just the private pilot," Imani continued.

"And what makes you think you succeeded?" another pilot asked.

Imani responded without hesitation, "The number of midair collisions and near misses is down by ten percent."

"So is the number of private planes," the pilot shot back.

"Those are non-high-performance aircraft," Imani replied, unruffled.

"We can't all trade our tractors in for Corvettes, ma'am," the pilot retorted, eliciting laughter.

Another voice boomed from the back, "If things are so good now, why do you want to improve them? Regs are tight enough, don't you think?"

"I won't argue with that," Imani responded to some relieved chuckles from the group.

A heckler from the crowd couldn't resist. "She won't answer it either."

The first pilot approached the podium. "But, Madam Chairman, you still haven't told us how this fancy computer system will make things safer. Sounds to me like it's just one more way the government can butt its nose into someplace it doesn't belong."

"I don't have to remind you that the government runs the control towers in this country," Imani replied firmly.

"I wouldn't say that too loudly, ma'am," he countered. "Seems everyone remembers how the controllers did with that PSA flight a few years back. No slight against you, ma'am, or the fine work your agency has been doing. Recently, that is."

Imani looked to Lester for support, but she was on her own in this confrontation.

The approach controller skillfully operated a switch in the control tower, studying the conflict matrix with a concerned expression. The request from Japan Airlines had thrown a wrench into the otherwise smooth flow of air traffic. Demands filled the tower, echoing the Japanese pilot's, each one a ripple in the sea of control.

"American 460 maintain 7,000. Reduce airspeed to 230 knots. Contact tower 118.3. Delta two one eight, descend and maintain flight level two zero. Report abeam Mission Bay VOR," he rattled off with rapid precision.

Turning his attention to the Japanese pilot, he offered a correction, "Japan 719, information is Romeo. One eight four six Greenwich weather. Two zero thousand and scattered. Visibility two zero. Temperature six-four, dew point 4.2. Wind zero seven zero at one zero. Altimeter 3.024. VFR approach in use for runway 27. Say altitude."

"Oh, sorry. Flight level uh three two uh zero," came the apologetic response from the JAL pilot.

Frustration lining his voice, the controller fired back, "JAL 719 heavy, squawk 6925. Make immediate left turn heading one seven zero. Descend and maintain one five. Report over the course." He clicked off the mic with a sharp movement.

There was a pause before the Japan pilot's voice broke the

silence again, a misunderstanding lacing his words. "Squawk 6925 down to one seven over the golf course, 719."

The thin man sighed, pinching the bridge of his nose. The next few minutes promised to be a challenging ballet of correcting course and managing the other incoming flights.

2

A pilot and several others rose from their seats in the meeting room. "And Ma'am, we have a brief presentation, a kind of token of our appreciation for you being here. Something you might want to take back to Washington with you," he stated with a sly grin.

With a snap of his fingers, the lights went out. A few men carried in what looked like an upside-down wedding cake made of cardboard. "This is a model of the traffic control area in San Diego. Jets can come in up here at twenty thousand feet, slice right through here down to the field. Piece of cake."

Two men clad in white chef coats entered as he finished, carrying an actual wedding cake. They decorated the cake with a control tower and a couple of model planes seemingly on a collision course. They set it next to the cardboard model, its candles flickering under the artificial lights of the room.

Imani's smile was more strained now, the light-hearted atmosphere giving way to a sense of mockery.

"But our little planes, well, we got to scoot in down here at the bottom," he continued. His tone was sour, and his words were met with grumbles of agreement from the audience.

A heckler called, "Yeah, and how the hell are we supposed to fly if the FAA and the NTSB cut us out of these damn meetings?"

Another pilot interrupted, "My wife found your notice in the obituary column of The Examiner."

"Gentlemen, let's have some order, please. Chairman Safe will only be with us for a few short hours today. We should appreciate her taking the time out of her busy schedule to come all the way from Washington to see us," said Lester.

The room resettled after Lester's plea for order. The lead pilot cleared his throat and continued. "So the way we see it, we private pilots got to make a wish and hope for the best."

With a deep breath, he made a wish and blew out the candles. "Because if we let the FAA go ahead with their plan, our air traffic system will look like this."

With a dramatic flourish, the men in chef coats flipped the cake upside down, splattering icing all over the speaker's table. "And gentlemen, you and I will be licking it off the floor."

The room erupted into an uproar, the meeting devolving into chaos. Amidst the sea of icing-covered planes, the tiny tower stood erect, a lone symbol of the airspace they fought for.

On the runway, the wheels of a landing 747 smoked against the hot tarmac.

Inside the buzzing control tower, Imani and Lester entered. "I didn't come here to be insulted by a bunch of flying yahoos, Lester," Imani stated sternly.

"But they liked you, Chairman. It's just their way of showing it," Lester replied, attempting to placate her. "They're trying to get Washington's attention. Make a statement," he added, his voice hoarse.

Imani grabbed a phone from the center console and dialed. Her gaze flickered around the room, landing on the tower controller. She saw something, an inconsistency perhaps, and set the phone down, advancing towards the thin man with a purpose in her stride.

Imani moved to his station and rapidly scanned the screens, flight levels, and cluttered notes.

"Something wrong?" he asked, his gaze darting between the screens and the imposing figure of the NTSB chairman.

"Have you got American 460 on the inbound?" Imani asked, her tone serious.

He quickly pointed to a blip on one screen. "Right there. On a five-mile final."

"And where's the flight from Japan?" Imani queried further.

"Number two after the Delta," he replied, pointing at another blip.

Imani's gaze lingered on the screen, a frown creasing her forehead. "Japan is too high. If you don't cut American's descent, their landing gear'll slice through the Japan cabin. You'll have teriyaki all over the runway."

Taken aback by Imani's stark words, the controller reassessed the situation. She was right. He quickly grabbed the mic and barked, "American 460 maintain seven thousand. Offset to the right without further delay."

A voice crackled over the radio, "Four six zero."

Without a moment's pause, he continued, "Japan 719 descend to thirty-five hundred. Offset to the left without further delay."

Another voice acknowledged the command, "Down to three-five, Seven One Niner."

From her vantage point, Imani could see the two planes veer away from each other in the afternoon sky, narrowly avoiding a catastrophic mid-air collision.

Back in the tower, the harried controller wiped his brow, a

visible sign of relief washing over him. "Thanks," he murmured, a hint of embarrassment creeping into his voice.

As the radio buzzed with another pilot's voice, "Lindbergh Tower, Delta two one eight on final," the controller took a deep breath. "Two one eight cleared to land runway two-seven. Wind 230 at 14. Caution wind shear and wake turbulence on landing," he responded, trying to steady his shaky voice.

However, the requests kept coming, the next one from a Citation pilot, "Cessna 65 Lima at 27, ready for takeoff. Request northbound departure."

On the taxiway, two passenger jets whined behind a Citation lining up for takeoff. High above, a Delta jet skimmed the tops of buildings, its flaps lowered and gear down, thundering in on its final descent. From this distance, you could see the rivets holding them in place.

The interior of the control tower hummed with tension. Imani kept a wary eye on the controller as he tried to regain his composure.

"Six-five Lima, no delay, clear for immediate takeoff. Contact San Diego Radio on 122.4 after you depart the TCA," his voice crackled through the microphone, firm despite the underlying weariness.

Imani turned to him, curious, knitting her eyebrows together. "Have you been on for long today?"

"Sixteen hours. The head guy called in sick. Something going around," he confessed, eyes barely leaving the screen.

Outside, at the edge of the runway, a Cessna Citation roared to life, its jets firing with intensity as it hurtled along the tarmac.

. . .

Back inside the tower, he hastily crossed off the departing jet from his worksheet. He sighed heavily. "My wife's having a baby," he mentioned offhand, his tone a mix of fatigue and excitement.

Imani listened intently while still gazing at the incoming and outgoing flights.

"Japan 719 cleared to land. Wind 210 at 13. Follow the Delta. Delta two one eight contact ground on 123.9," he relayed the instructions.

Down on the runway, the wheels of a landing Delta smoked rubber as they slammed onto the runway at a blinding one hundred and forty miles an hour.

Inside the tower, Imani let out a breath she hadn't realized she'd been holding. Looking over at the controller, she asked, "Boy or girl?"

"We hope it's a girl," he replied, a small smile breaking through his exhaustion.

Daylight streamed across the runway, illuminating the screeching tires of the Japan flight as they smoked onto the tarmac, a full payload in tow. Moments later, the American tires followed suit, rolling to a halt with the same grace as their predecessor. Nearby, another set of jet wheels contacted the ground, reverse thrusters hissing along the centerline.

3

In the control tower, Imani returned to the center desk, her fingers lightly dancing over the phone's buttons. As observant as ever, her eyes watched the controllers as she dialed a number. She perked up as the call connected.

"Hi. How's my day going? Well, you remember Aunt Nia's fifth wedding, the one to the birdwatcher who brought his homing pigeons to the reception? Worse."

In a San Francisco office tower, Imani's husband, Orville Safe, sat amidst the humdrum of paperwork. In his early fifties, Orville would make a classic research scientist look like a playboy. Copies of Golf magazine rested on the table.

"Why don't we get away for a few days? Go to Palm Springs. Play some golf. How about it?" he suggested, his voice a soothing lull in Imani's chaotic day.

"When did you get interested in golf?" Imani queried, surprise lacing her words.

Orville chuckled softly. "You sound like you could use the time off, and I'd be willing to learn."

"That's sweet of you, Orville. Do you want to meet there?"

"No. I'll fly down. Take you to a nice dinner at the Del. Have a leisurely drive through the desert. And you can howl at the coyotes."

"Sounds romantic," she said.

"See you in a couple of hours."

"Orville, wait. What airline are you flying?" Imani asked.

"Whichever one has a seat. It's Friday afternoon."

Back in the control tower, Imani held the phone close, her eyes scanning the airspace outside the windows. "I'll check on the kids. Love you," she said before hanging up.

She turned to the FAA Director. "Your tower controller is burned out, Les. You should get him off the desk," she advised Lester, who was reviewing the work schedule.

"I've got three guys out with this flu. What am I supposed to do?" Lester defended his decision.

"I'll work the desk. Whatever it takes," Imani offered, resolute.

"You can't do that. You're the headman," he protested.

"Yeah, I'm the headman," Imani scoffed.

Lester turned to another controller. "Butler, can you relieve Martino?"

A young kid hustled into the tower controller's station, breaking the tension between Imani and Lester.

"You had a near miss, Lester." Imani was firm.

"But Chairman, Miramar field averages thirteen conflict alerts a day."

"One is too many," Imani reiterated, referencing the near miss. "I want a full report before I leave."

·   ·   ·

Later, a phone ringing echoed through a children's bedroom in Washington, D.C. The nanny on duty answered it while putting Darius, a five-year-old boy, to bed.

"Hello? Oh, hello, Mrs. Safe. Yes, we're okay, but I'm afraid we have some bad news for you," she informed.

Back in the control tower, Imani took a seat, her face paling at the words on the other end of the line.

"What's wrong, Dotty?" she asked, a note of trepidation sneaking into her voice.

As evening draped its veil over the day, the nanny in the children's bedroom gently removed a thermometer from Darius's mouth. Tiny beads of sweat gathered on his forehead, a stark contrast against his fever-flushed skin. Red splotches appeared, dotting his hands and neck like a morbid constellation.

"I think Darius has measles," the nanny relayed, concern lacing her words.

"Does he have a temperature?" Imani's voice echoed from the speakerphone.

"Looks that way."

"Have you called the doctor?" Imani asked.

"I was going to do that right now."

"Let me talk to him."

With a gentle hand, the nanny passed the phone to the perspiring boy.

"Hi, Mom. I got measles from that new girl in music class," Darius said, his voice weak yet tinged with a note of accusation.

"I guess you'll miss your violin lessons, won't you?" Imani tried to keep her tone light despite the concern eating at her.

"Hope so. When are you and Dad coming home?" Darius asked, his words punctuated by the yearning in his voice.

Imani paused for a moment, swallowing the lump in her throat. "First thing in the morning, honey. Is your sister there?"

"No, Dotty won't let her come near me. She says I'll contaminate her."

"Well, you wouldn't want to do that, would you?" Imani tried to inject humor into the situation but failed to lighten the mood.

"Maybe," came the faintly cheeky reply from Darius.

In the control tower, bathed in the dying daylight, Imani whispered soothing words to her son.

"Listen, get some sleep, and do what Dotty and the doctor tell you, okay? Love you," she said, pressing the phone closer as if she could reach through it to comfort her ailing son. She felt a pang of helplessness and yearning to be there, holding him close, but for now, she had to make do with just a voice through the phone.

4

——————

High in the afternoon sky over Mexico, a Lear 35 jet streaked through the clouds, dancing an aerial waltz. It gracefully executed a lazy-8, a figure eight maneuver on a 45-degree plane before pitching upwards in a bold chandelle, a steep climb and turn.

Inside the jet, the instrument panel was like a video game of motion and light. At an altitude of twenty-five thousand feet, dials spun, needles twitched, and lights flickered on the jet.

"Wouldn't want to have a vacuum failure at this attitude, would we, Wilbur?" came a voice brimming with bravado. Y. Fraser Gillingham, in his early fifties. Handsome, successful, and teeming with relentless confidence, he was a risk-taker with fire dancing in his eyes. Seated comfortably on the left side of the cockpit, he had a firm grip on the controls.

"No, sir, we wouldn't," responded Captain Wilbur, a man in his mid-sixties wearing a full airline uniform. Seated on his hands, he starkly contrasted his enthusiastic companion.

"Doing pretty good, aren't I, Wilbur?" Fraser asked, glancing over with a cocky grin.

"You're a real pro, sir," Wilbur complimented, albeit through gritted teeth.

"Ah, you're just bullshitting me," Fraser laughed. "Ever spin one of these?"

"No, sir. I don't think that would be a good idea," Wilbur warned, his eyes fixed on the gauges' wild dance.

"It can take it, though, right? The manual says so." Fraser, unfazed, pulled back on the yoke, a grin stretching across his face. Suddenly, a stall warning echoed through the flight deck. The stick shuddered under Fraser's grip, yet he merely laughed, unfazed. "Love the feel of two Gs in my gut, don't you?"

Wilbur, barely breathing, gasped, "Yes, sir."

"Tell me when we hit ten thousand," Fraser ordered, his eyes on the view outside the window.

"You're not watching the altimeter, sir?" Wilbur asked, his voice straining with concern.

"And miss a pretty girl on the beach?" Fraser replied, his gaze seemingly more focused on the ground below than the plummeting altitude. The altimeter needle spun wildly, indicating a descent rate of two thousand feet per minute. "Yahoo!"

Outside, the Lear jet spiraled through the afternoon sky, nosediving through the fluffy clouds. It spun like a top, a dazzling and terrifying spectacle against the vast blue expanse.

A light blinked on the flight deck of the Lear jet. At the exact moment, the phone rang. Still, in a steep dive, the men shared a glance of disbelief.

"Who'd be calling at a time like this?" the thrill-seeking pilot quipped, keeping a firm grip on the yoke.

"I'll get it." The captain, still breathless from the spinning descent, reached to connect.

"Hello. He's right here. It's for you, sir. Icarus."

The plane continued to spin, but Fraser, in charge, merely smirked. "Tell him I'm indisposed for the moment."

"Mr. Gillingham will be right with you." The captain relayed the message, keeping his voice steady despite the disorienting spin.

With practiced finesse, Fraser pulled out of the spin.

Outside, the Lear jet executed one last graceful roll before resuming straight-and-level flight.

Fraser brushed his thinning hair casually and said to the captain, "She's all yours."

In the cabin, two women - one blonde, one brunette, both barely out of their teens - clung to airsickness bags, their complexions a ghastly white. "Told you flying was fun," Fraser said, smirking at their discomfort. He picked up his coffee, still hot and miraculously unspilled, then settled behind a desk and switched on the speakerphone.

"Hell of a time to be calling the boss, Sam," he chided, his voice clear over the speaker.

"I wouldn't do it if it weren't important, Mr. Gillingham," came the apologetic reply.

"So what have you got? A pregnant mother or a terrorist threat?" he asked, leaning back in his seat with an air of amusement.

Meanwhile, at the San Francisco airport's pilot-ready room, pilots diligently checked their flight plans. "It's Finicky, sir. He won't fly 86 to San Diego," said the Director of Operations, Sam Icarus.

"Something wrong with San Diego? I thought he lived here," said Fraser over the phone.

"It's not the city, sir. It's the plane. I'm going to tell him if he doesn't do the flight, I'll send him to Alaska, and he can walk back."

"Just give him something else?"

"There is nothing else," Icarus replied.

"You mean to tell me out of our fleet of six hundred and thirty-nine fine aircraft, you can't find one goddamned bird the good captain will fly?"

"He's threatened to go to the union, sir. It's his last flight. He retires tomorrow. He said he wanted to talk to you."

"Put him on."

After shuffling on the line, a familiar voice broke in. "This is Captain Finicky, sir. I wouldn't fly that deathtrap if it were the last one on earth."

"Why not?" Fraser asked.

"It's fifteen hours past TBO, sir."

"Fifteen? Did I hear you correctly, Captain?"

"Yes sir, fifteen hours past its time before overhaul."

"That is serious. Fifteen, right?"

"Yes, sir," Finicky replied.

As the Lear continued its flight, Fraser paused, his gaze thoughtful. "Captain, you know how sometimes when your car is due for an oil change, and you don't get right to it at six thousand miles like it says to do in the owner's manual?" he asked, his voice casual.

The blonde woman moved towards Fraser, carrying a glass of scotch. He accepted it with a nod, still holding the captain's attention.

"I don't know if it's ever happened to you, but it's happened to me once or twice," he continued, his words smooth. "And maybe it goes over just a little, sometimes ten thousand, perhaps even twenty. The car still runs, right?"

The blonde woman slid into Fraser's open arms, her face alight with adoration. He accepted her warmth without a pause, his words never faltering. "They make them that way because they know not everybody will change the oil every six thousand miles. Know what I mean?"

He spared a second to glance down at the woman who had started gnawing on his earlobe. "Same thing with airplanes. A couple of hours one way or the other never hurt anything?"

The brunette joined them, her hands reaching to unbutton his shirt and then beginning to massage his chest at twenty thousand feet.

"Listen, I'm glad you brought this to my attention," he said, a smile tugging at his lips. "The dedication and professionalism of pilots like you make me proud to be running this airline. I'll tell you. It hurts me to think we'll be losing one of our best when you retire tomorrow."

He paused, his eyes lighting up with a sudden idea. "Tell you what. When you get to San Diego, let me take you and your pretty wife to dinner. It'd be a treat for me. What do you say?"

"Sir, I've been with this airline for thirty-five years. It'd be an honor, Mr. Gillingham." The reply came through the speaker, laden with respect.

"Call me Fraser, Captain," the boss responded, his voice soft yet firm.

"Thank you, sir." The line clicked off.

Grinning, Fraser poured a tequila shooter and raised his glass in a toast to the two women in his arms. "You just got to know how to grease the wheels," he winked, his laughter mixing with the hum of the plane's engines.

5

The afternoon sun streamed down on the bustling San Francisco Airport airline ticket counter. Amidst the hum of activity, Orville was stuck in a slow-moving line, his impatience growing with each passing minute. He anxiously checked his watch while the ticket agent tagged and sent the suitcases into the airport conveyor belt system.

Outside, the luggage found itself in the competent yet rough hands of the baggage handlers. Racing to keep up with the relentless rhythm of departures and arrivals, they loaded the baggage onto a waiting cart, its wheels groaning in protest. Amidst their haste, a garment bag slipped from their grasp and fell prey to the relentless tread of a tire.

The handlers were soon heaving the surviving luggage into the hold of a Boeing 737. They worked with the efficiency of repetition and a lack of time, even as handles snapped and bags tore. Despite the minor casualties, they kept tossing, forming a symphony of organized chaos.

. . .

Inside the Boeing, a cleaning crew hustled, matching their counterparts outside. They vacuumed, emptied trash cans, cleared ashtrays, and replaced the kitchen trays. The lingering smell of stale smoke suggested a time when smoking was an accepted norm within these confines.

Beneath them, an engineer wrestled with draining the toilets in the less glamorous parts of the plane. As a mouse skittered across the carpet, the accompanying trainee wrinkled his nose in disgust; his sentiments mirrored in his words. "This job stinks," he complained. His companion merely shrugged in reply. "What do you expect?"

Back outside, the cleaning crew hurried out of the plane, their places quickly taken by an ARA services truck. It backed up to the plane, its machinery whirring as it hoisted a fresh supply of food and drinks.

During all this activity, the flight engineer carried out his pre-flight walk around the plane with a clipboard and flashlight. As he methodically checked each aspect of the aircraft, the fuel truck began pumping jet fuel into the wing tanks.

"Don't forget to check under the hood," the flight engineer called out to a mechanic, who reported a problem. "You got a slow leak in a port tire. Take an hour to replace it."

The flight engineer offered a compromise with a dismissive wave: "You got ten minutes. Patch it."

The team's efficient and determined work resembled a well-rehearsed pit crew, showcasing the organization of airline ground operations. Cranking, cleaning, filling, emptying, loading, pumping, and checking.

.   .   .

The Boeing 737 flight deck buzzed with activity as the engineer settled into his seat. Outside, the rhythmic sweeps of a window washer cleared the windshield's distorted view of the world. Captain Finicky, focused on the flight plan in his hands, inquired over his shoulder, "Everything okay?"

The engineer quipped back, the humor a thin veneer over his focused diligence, "Aside from the facelift and the cheap perfume." A thumbs-up sign from the window wiper assured Finicky that, despite the jests, everything was in order. "Let's get this show on the road. I'm meeting the big cheese." He smiled.

Meanwhile, at the San Francisco International's ticket counter, Orville finally stepped up to the counter. His urgent request for a ticket to San Diego was met with a routine inquiry.

"Can I see your ticket, please?" The agent asked.

"I don't have one yet," he admitted.

"So, you want to go standby?" The ticket agent offered. Orville nodded in affirmation, his desperate gaze fixed on the terminal screen.

"The next flight leaves in an hour and a half. Is that okay?" the agent inquired, only to be met with a frustrated sigh. "I don't want to wait any longer," he complained. The agent explained, "I'm sorry, sir, but this flight is fully booked." Orville felt down but decided to look for other options.

Night had fallen when Orville reached the crowded boarding area. As the boarding staff announced over the P.A. system that all passengers for the San Diego flight should be on board, Orville muscled his way forward. "I need to get on this flight," he insisted, prompting the clerk to jot down his name.

"Last call for standby passenger, Harry Pasternak. Party of three," the check-in agent announced over the P.A. system. A frazzled family claimed their boarding passes.

"Go right aboard," the agent said.

"Thank you. Thank you."

The man and his wife dragged their child down the jetway. When the agent returned from the ramp, he said, "That's it. Close it off."

Orville tried again to secure a seat. "You must have *one* seat available," he pleaded, only to be met with a polite but firm denial. "I'm sorry, sir. The flight is full."

"But you don't understand. I'm supposed to meet my wife," Orville tried to explain.

The check-in agent informed him. "There's another flight at nine." She told him.

Orville calmed himself down. "Look, I know how you over-book sometimes, and I know you keep telling me this flight is full, but I'm meeting my wife in San Diego. Imani Safe, Chairman of the NTSB. Maybe you've heard of her?"

The agent took him more seriously now. His credentials struck a chord with her.

"Now, I'm going to go over there and sit down for a minute, and you see what you can do. I'd really like to get on this flight," he said.

Orville retired to a row of chairs while the agent and clerk discussed his case. He flipped open a copy of Scientific American. Orville straightened his tie. The agent and the passenger handling agent exchanged whispers. The boarding agent got on the phone. A moment passed.

The boarding staff announced over the PA system, "Passengers bound for San Diego, Flight 860 will be delayed."

Undeterred, Orville approached the counter, pressing for details on the delay.

"How long is the delay?" He asked.

"It shouldn't be long."

"What's wrong?"

"Nothing, Mr. Safe."

"So why aren't you going, then?"

A busy passenger exited the jetway, baggage in tow. "You want to know a faster way to San Diego? Walk."

"What did they say?" Orville asked the man.

The departing passenger spoke in hushed tones, offering a cryptic hint. "These people don't exactly volunteer information, but I've clocked enough miles to know that if there's a mouse in a food locker, you're bound to find a rat."

He moved off just as Captain Finicky arrived, introduced himself, and shook Orville's hand.

"Mr. Safe. I'm Captain Finicky, the pilot in command. Glad to have you aboard, sir. Welcome to Paragon."

"Well, thank you." Orville was relieved.

"We had a little difficulty with the flight clearance, sir, but it should just be a matter of minutes before we're underway," Captain Finicky informed him.

After a baggage handler took his bags and Orville shot a satisfied grin at the boarding staff, he was finally led aboard the plane.

The Boeing 737's first-class cabin buzzed with the murmur of hushed conversations and the faint rustle of duty-free shopping bags. Amidst the packed crowd, the flight attendant expertly stowed away the passengers' luggage.

"I'd invite you up to the flight deck," Captain Finicky said to Orville, his voice balancing regret and obligation, "but we're almost ready to taxi, and it would be against regulations."

Orville only chuckled. "That's fine. I just wanted to meet my wife sometime before midnight." His casual remark masked the urgency of his wish.

Orville quickly requested a change when asked if his current seat was satisfactory. "I prefer to sit closer to the back by the emergency exit," he said, deftly retrieving his briefcase before following the flight attendant to his new location. "I need the legroom."

A sense of relief washed over Orville as they entered the main cabin. Seeing a couple of kids donning Mickey Mouse hats and eagerly sipping on their Cokes brought a hint of a smile to his face. One kid, bolder than the rest, sneakily swiped a sandwich from the food locker.

Orville settled into his seat by the emergency exit, the briefcase in his lap. "I usually work when I fly," he said as the flight attendant offered to take the case. With a polite smile, he was left to his own devices as the flight attendant promised assistance at the ring of a bell.

On the flight deck, Captain Finicky, the copilot, and the engineer busied themselves with the pre-flight check. The familiar voice of Ground Control punctuated their tasks. "Paragon 860, you are clear to the apron. Taxi into position for two eight left and hold," the voice announced.

"Finally," Finicky exhaled, his hand firing the thrusters while the copilot acknowledged the instructions. "Two eight left, 860."

Back in the main cabin, Orville was deep in his own world. His wallet was in his hand, revealing a cherished family picture of his wife, Imani, and their kids. As he lost himself in the warm memory, the aircraft shuddered into motion, the engines' increasing roar indicating the beginning of the journey.

.   .   .

Outside, the sprawling San Francisco International's runway
28L was the stage for the Boeing 737's graceful debut. The
Paragon flight positioned itself on the threshold, revved, and
took off.

From the tower, the controller's voice gave the all-clear,
"Paragon 860 cleared to the Papa beacon, straight out departure. Climb and maintain flight level nine zero. Proceed
heading zero six zero until intercepting the 325 radial from the
Oakland VOR."

With these words, the plane's tires kissed the ground goodbye, lifting off the runway and into the dark canvas of the
night sky.

6

The low hum of the Boeing 737's engines droned on in the dimly lit cabin. Orville sat by the window, transfixed by the rhythmic motion of the vast wing shaking in the stiff breeze. The strobe lights flashed on the dark foil, and the spoiler performed a captivating dance for the passenger.

With a familiar chime, the 'Fasten Seatbelt' sign turned off. Orville, however, kept his on, only loosening it for comfort. Beside him, a short, rotund man stretched his legs, noticing Orville's still-fastened belt.

"You going to keep that on?" he asked, eyeing the belt curiously.

"Might hit a microburst. Bounce off the cabin. Crack your skull," Orville replied without missing a beat.

"Oh." The man's eyebrows knitted together, processing the unusual response.

"I'm a scientist," Orville continued, his voice laced with a hint of pride. "My brain is the only thing I've got." With that, he resumed his reading of Scientific American. A bit taken aback by potential airborne calamities, his seatmate nonchalantly refastened his seatbelt.

Meanwhile, the Lear Jet touched down at the private terminal FBO at San Diego Airport. Fraser stepped off the plane into the night, leaving behind the familiar hum of the aircraft.

Back on the Boeing 737, the cabin crew was bustling about, collecting empty food trays and glasses from passengers. The 'Fasten Seatbelt' sign repeated, prompting a flight attendant to announce. "Ladies and gentlemen, the captain has turned on the fasten seatbelt sign. We'll be landing in San Diego in just a few minutes. Temperature is sixty-eight degrees, and we expect a light drizzle when we arrive." She adjusted her blouse as another flight attendant squeezed past her in the aisle.

"Passengers requiring assistance leaving the aircraft should remain in their seats until we reach the jetway. A flight attendant will help you. We hope you've had a pleasant flight, and on behalf of Captain Finicky and the crew, we thank you for flying the friendly skies of Paragon. Welcome to San Diego."

Throughout the announcement, Orville's face remained impassive yet focused, a warmth in his eyes hinting at his affable nature. As classical music filled his ears, he finished his beer and reached down to rotate the channel selector on his radio. The music cut out, replaced by the crackling voice of Captain Finicky.

"Lindbergh Approach, Paragon 860 with you out of two eight zero with information Echo," the captain's voice echoed through the radio, connecting Orville to the flight deck from his seat in the cabin.

. . .

In the belly of the night, the flight deck of the Boeing 737 was bathed in a soft, artificial glow. The approach controller's voice filtered through the cockpit speakers, "Paragon 860, your traffic is a Mooney, three miles out at eleven o'clock and a DC-10 below at one. Turn heading zero seven zero. Correction, zero eight zero for an ILS approach Runway 30R. Descend to seven thousand five hundred. Report abeam the Mission Bay VOR. Good night."

"Traffic in sight. Down to seven five heading zero eight zero. Paragon 860," Captain Finicky responded crisply. But then, without warning, a loud thud resonated against the jet's body, shaking the seasoned pilots.

"What was that?" Finicky demanded, his eyes narrowing.

"A bird?" the copilot offered, though his voice quivered uncertainly.

"Sounded like a car door," the flight engineer retorted, grimacing at the strange, unsettling sound.

Through his window, Orville gaped at the wild dance of the wing, its rhythmic sway replaced with violent tremors as the plane plunged through the clouds. Then another slam echoed around him, a horrifying symphony of tearing metal and something, impossibly, being chewed up.

Inside the main cabin, chaos unfurled. Hurricane winds spilled into the cabin. The floor thirty feet in front of Orville ripped apart, a gaping maw opening to the screaming winds outside. The cabin depressurized, triggering a torrent of oxygen masks from the overhead compartments. Panic reigned as the passengers were thrust into a nightmarish reality.

Back on the flight deck, Finicky wrestled with the yoke. "Mayday, Mayday, Mayday. Lindbergh. Paragon 860 twenty northwest inbound. Speed 320. Flight level one six zero. Request emergency landing. Call the equipment. We're going down." His voice was fraught with urgency over the stick shaker's rattle and the stall warning's shriek. The copilot called, "We've been hit."

The engineer said, "Easy baby, easy baby, get the nose down."

While the cabin descended into pandemonium, Orville remained an island of calm amidst the storm. He slipped on his oxygen mask, tightened his seatbelt, secured his briefcase, and clutched his seat cushion, all while a macabre dance of terror played out around him.

The stick shaker rattled, and the stall warning shrieked.

"Get the damn nose down and give me full power. I'm bringing her in," Finicky shouted. As Captain Finicky and the copilot valiantly battled to land the crippled aircraft, a sense of doom crept into the engineer's voice. "We're dead, man. This is it."

Undeterred, Finicky issued a string of orders. "Flaps ten. Shut down number one. It's burning."

"Mom, I love you," mouthed the copilot.

In the tower, the controller uttered, "Paragon 860's in trouble. They're squawking 7700." The inexperienced controller was submerged in a sea of emergency procedures, simultaneously handling multiple phones, screens, and radios. "Paragon, the equipment's on the way. You are cleared for a straight-in approach runway 275. Wind two seven zero at one three," he relayed, even as he dialed the fire station's hotline.

"Got a loaded 737 coming in hard. Give me everything you've got and call the hospital. It's going to be a long night." With those grim words, he began rerouting inbound traffic, snapping commands into the mic, orchestrating a chaotic ballet in the night sky above.

ATC snapped, "I've rerouted the inbound to Miramar."

The young controller pressed on. "PSA Two One Five depart the runway without further delay. Delta Seven Zero Niner execute immediate go-around. Contact departure 125.9. Western Two Eight go-round. Shit."

7

The airport was a hive of activity, a discordance of wailing sirens punctuated by the thunderous roar of jet engines. Amidst this chaotic concerto, Lester barged into the control tower.

"What's going on?" he demanded, his gaze darting from one anxious face to another.

"We've got Paragon inbound with a problem," the controller responded, his voice tight with stress.

"What's the nature of the emergency?" Lester quizzed, his heart pounding in rhythm with the flashing lights outside.

A western pilot on the radio crackled in, "Tower, Western two eight, we see a ball of fire up ahead. Heading change to one eight zero."

"Engine failure," was the terse reply, followed by a crackle on the radio. "Western Two Eight, clear to one eight zero. Says he's hit. Looks bad."

"Get him back on," said Lester.

"Paragon 860, Lindbergh ATC, you are now eight miles from the airport. State your status, sir," the young controller spoke up.

The tower held its collective breath as the plane approached. Then, with a casual air that belied the gravity of the situation, Fraser Gillingham and his Lear pilot entered. Assessed the situation, He'd seen it all before. Lester recognized him instantly.

"I was in the neighborhood," Fraser said, a concerned look in his eye. "Heard one of my birds was in distress."

The room vibrated with a cacophony of shouts and orders. Through it all, the pilot's voice trembled over the transmission. "Gonna' try to bring the lady in. Down to six five zero. She's spinning like shit. We've lost all elevator control. Stabilizers gone. Number one engine's on fire. Try to ditch in the ocean. -- Tell Beth I love her."

The air traffic controller turned to Lester. "Sir, we have visual contact."

He painted a grim picture. The plane spun wildly out of control, the elevator and stabilizer were gone.

With growing dread, Fraser and Lester took turns with the binoculars, their eyes tracking the ball of fire that was once a state-of-the-art airliner.

"Poor bastards," Fraser muttered, passing the binoculars back to Lester.

The controller tried to maintain radio contact. "Paragon 860, we're right with you. You are off the profile. How do you read 860?" No answer. "Paragon 860, turn heading zero eight zero. Tailwind shifting now to 320 at one eight."

"Last thing they need is an unstable wind," said Lester.

The flight controller continued, "Paragon, you are clear for Runway two seven five. Do you have gear, Paragon? -- One two three four five, Paragon. Is your landing gear working? Squawk 8700."

He looked at the radar. No change. Fraser quietly took the mic from the controller and set the headset on the table.

Then, breaking the near reverent silence, Imani walked in.

She looked at Fraser, and he looked back, an electric charge passing between them. It was a gaze that spoke of a shared history, a long and storied past.

It was as though the world stopped for a moment.

"Hello, Fraser," Imani said, her voice calm and composed. "Whenever I see you, it's a disaster."

Fraser acknowledged, a pleasant grin on his face. "Well, Chairman Safe, I don't suppose you're here to tour the wild animal park," he said.

They shared a momentary look of recognition that revealed a deep and painful past between them.

Before Imani could respond, the sky to the west exploded with light, and the ground beneath their feet shuddered violently. It was an explosion far off but unmistakably devastating.

"I've seen enough wild animals in my time," Imani said, keeping her gaze on Fraser.

"Then it's the passionate call of the wild."

The tower seemed to quiet for a moment, and both Imani and Fraser knew what they needed to do. Neither relished what they knew they were about to face, but tragedy was something that they had been trained for in many ways. Imani headed for the stairs.

"It's dangerous out there," Fraser cautioned.

"It's dangerous everywhere," she said.

Fraser responded grimly, gesturing for her to lead the way. A palpable hush settled over the control room as they walked out of the tower together. The chaotic sounds of the night dimmed under the weight of the tragic catastrophe that had just unfolded.

They rushed down the stairs. The clamor of the fire station filled the air as a firefighter provided them with Newtex fire entry suits and headgear. As they wriggled into the suits, Fraser remarked, "I swear to God you're the last person I expected to see here."

"I thought nothing ever surprised you," Imani replied.

"Only you, Imani," Fraser responded, his gaze intense. "Only you could bring this level of excitement into my life."

"Have I done something I don't know about?" Imani asked, betraying her concern.

Fraser rolled his eyes and gathered up his courage. "When you ran out on me, you broke my heart, and you didn't even kiss me goodbye."

"Hard to do when we were both drowning," she replied. She turned to the firefighter. "Can you zip me up?"

"Love to," Fraser smiled.

But she snubbed him, and before Fraser could respond, a firefighter who had helped them secure their gear interrupted them. Fraser's disappointment was evident, but he swallowed it and moved on.

"Sure you wanna do this?" Fraser asked.

"I need to be close to the action."

"You don't have to," he said.

She dismissed his comment. "What are we waiting for?" Imani asked, ready for action. She climbed onto the jump seat of the fire truck. The engine roared to life, and two Dalmatians hopped in beside the driver. There was no room for Fraser. With a shrug, he said, "I always knew I'd get to play fireman someday." And with that, he jumped onto the back of the truck, holding on for dear life as they sped off.

The debris field spread for miles, along the runway, beyond the tarmac, out to the ocean.

A bank of fire trucks trained water hoses on the flaming wreckage. The crash site was a living nightmare. Flames roared and danced around the plane's skeleton, fed by gusts of wind that ignited the grass and fanned the inferno. Rescuers, already hard at work, directed water hoses at the wreckage, spraying chemical flame retardants and using their tools to reach any survivors.

The fire truck slowed, and they jumped off.

"Time to enter hell," Fraser muttered, pulling his headgear on.

Imani watched the scene, and the scale of the disaster was more extensive than she had expected. She pulled her hair away from her face, donned her headgear, grabbed a flashlight, and joined Fraser. They stepped into the blazing inferno, the heat searing their faces even through their protective gear.

Scattered debris littered the area, each piece catching fire and contributing to the conflagration. Human bodies were strewn across the landscape, a chilling sight that froze Imani's heart. Blue and green flame everywhere, a terrible stench. Men shouting, radios crackling, stretchers arriving, sirens screaming.

Scattered aircraft parts flared up like brush fires as the wind redistributed the fire. Indistinguishable charred aircraft sections looked surreal as colored plastic melted into Daliesque pools.

They moved deeper into the disaster. Imani and Fraser looked like astronauts on a dystopian space walk.

Human bodies were strewn about the dark landscape. Imani found a perfectly intact Mickey Mouse hat among the wreckage and picked it up. Rescuers raced in behind her with wet blankets and tossed them on top of the screaming bodies.

Near the crushed nose of the plane, paramedics and fire-fighters, hard at work, moved survivors on stretchers out of the smoking wreckage. Fraser asked, "The Captain?"

"Sealed in. We're cutting him out now," a firefighter shouted as the jaws of life tore through the airplane skin, ready to extract the victims.

Fraser and Imani dove into the burning shell without wasting another moment, ready to risk their lives for those they might save.

8

A thick plume of smoke and the harsh smell of burning wreckage filled the flight deck. The rescue crew donned extrication suits and fought through the toxic fumes, using hydraulic cutters, spreaders, and rams to pry at the jammed flight deck door.

In the midst of them, Fraser's hands gripped a crowbar. He wedged it into the door's gap, heaving with all his might. The door creaked open, revealing the devastation within. Fraser shouldered his way inside. The sight that met him was grim. Fraser and Imani quickly checked for signs of life.

"He's breathing," Imani declared, her hands on Captain Finicky's neck. A firefighter joined her, and together, they lifted the captain out of the wreckage.

"And the other two?" a firefighter asked.

"Dead," Fraser replied, his gaze focused on the flight plan and instrument charts, which he quickly tucked inside a pouch in his suit. He ignored the flight engineer and co-pilot, diverting his attention to the floor.

. . .

Outside the wreckage, near the nose of the aircraft, an ambulance awaited the injured. Fraser emerged from the wreckage, and Imani rejoined the captain after aiding him.

"I'm going back in," she declared, her eyes burning with determination.

"The medics will get everyone else," Fraser assured her. But Imani was not to be deterred. "I want to help. There's got to be more alive," she insisted.

"Remember that fire we saw from the tower?" Fraser asked.

"What about it?"

"Probably dropped as much fuel as he could before he hit, but those reserve tanks could still blow." Fraser paused, reminding her of the imminent threat of exploding fuel tanks. "You want to add your name to the list of casualties?" he asked, his voice softer now.

"I have to do this," Imani replied, her resolve unwavering.

"Why?"

"It came in from SFO."

"So?"

"Exactly," Imani replied.

Fraser knew there was no stopping her. He climbed into the ambulance, giving her one last look before the vehicle sped away.

Chief Sparks, a burly firefighter, approached Imani. He was a veteran. His face hardened from countless fires, but the scene before him was one of the worst he'd ever seen.

"Chairman Safe?"

"Yes."

"I'm Chief Sparks. Helluva mess we got here tonight."

She nodded. In the heart of the crash site, Chief Sparks wiped the sweat from his brow, his grizzled face a testament to the pressure of the situation. "Worst I've seen in a long time," Chief Sparks said. He briefed Imani on the status.

"You have a headcount?" Imani asked.

"Manifest says close to two hundred, ma'am. Most burnt so bad take a dentist a month to identify them."

"But there are survivors?" She asked.

"Some." He admitted. "Help if we get that rain they keep forecasting. Be a goddamn act of God."

The Chief pointed off to the west. As Imani looked out onto the landscape, trails of raging flames stretched far into the distance. Firefighters battled to contain it. Over the ocean, a fog rolled in. Despite everything, Imani remained resolute, determined to help in any way she could.

"As long as we don't hit flash point with those tanks," he muttered. "Otherwise, I'd have to evacuate the men."

A messenger carrying news of a Coast Guard report interrupted his words.

"Sir, Coast Guard fireboats report passengers at sea. They're picking them up now," the messenger relayed, a hint of hopefulness in his voice.

"Survivors?" Chief Sparks asked, anticipation lining his question.

The messenger shook his head, replying, "None reported, sir."

The news hit Imani hard. She quickly instructed the messenger to keep her updated and moved away, only to face the grim sight of a coroner's van pulling in. Under the shroud of wet blankets, the tagged bodies were a harsh reminder of the tragedy.

"Chairman?" Chief Sparks called out, closing in on Imani. He handed her a walkie-talkie, advising her, "Take this. Do what you have to do." He then turned to a fire crew photographer, instructing him to stay with Imani.

Together, they moved through the disaster site, with Imani

leading the way through the wreckage that resembled a burning sculpture.

Imani walked through the hellish scene. As they progressed, a drizzle began and developed into a downpour, drenching the ground and the wreckage alike. The fog thickened and enveloped them. Thunder roared above. The sky opened up. Momentary relief washed over the firefighters as the torrent of water sizzled against the burning debris. The rain provided a respite from the blaze but transformed the crash site into a swamp of sorrow.

Whole sections of airline seats drenched in the pouring rain provided momentary relief to the exhausted firefighters. Medics paraded in more stretchers. Burning baggage and articles of clothing sizzled in the torrent.

Imani remained focused. She drew closer to the plane's wing, her flashlight illuminating the undamaged surface. The inboard spoilers were up. Flaps were down. Instructing the photographer to capture the sight, she inspected an engine, which was sunk into the muddy terrain. "Shoot that," she said.

The photographer fired off several shots of the wing. Imani moved in on the engines.

She got down on her hands and knees, scooping away the mud until the inside of the engine was visible. A chipped blade, a missing one. "Let's get this," she instructed, the photographer complying without hesitation.

As they continued their grim task, Imani's eyes traced a probable path from the engine pod through the pylon to the inboard flap. She noticed a small precision cut on the flap's trailing edge.

"I need one here," she directed, her voice firm despite the circumstances. The photographer obeyed, and they continued their journey through the wreckage, their path guided by the beam of Imani's flashlight.

"Get pictures of all the engines."

"Right."

When her inspection reached the rear emergency exit, she found the entire tail section was missing. The rain eased to a drizzle while the fog grew denser around them.

Imani turned on her walkie-talkie, the static filling the quiet air around them.

"Tower, this is Imani Safe. Do you read me, over?"

"This is the tower. Loud and clear. Over," came the voice.

"Did anyone call for me?"

"Seems like hundreds, Chairman. Press, TV crews, airport authority, the mayor, Secretary Dole. I expect the President any minute."

Then, her voice was barely above a whisper. "Did my husband call?"

A long pause followed before the reply came. "No, ma'am. Your husband did not call."

As the rain trickled down her face, mingling with unshed tears, she delivered one more instruction for the ill-fated flight. "I need the complete passenger manifest for this flight. Call me when you have it."

"Yes, ma'am. Ma'am?" came a query from the other end of the line. "Where are you?"

"In the field of despair," she replied, her voice breaking through the fog and the rain, echoing the grief of a disaster that had changed everything in one dreadful night. "Over and out."

9

On the beach, the flaming fuel trails stretched out to the sea, creating a vivid yet tragic spectacle as they burned up against the darkness. Fireboats and Coast Guard cutters circled the area, their lights cutting through the dense fog. The crashing waves echoed in the night as helicopters circled overhead, shining spotlights on the turbulent waters.

Imani stood alone, her gaze drawn to the ocean, her silhouette etched against the chaos and destruction. The walkie-talkie in her hand crackled to life, pulling her out of her thoughts.

"This is Lindbergh Tower to Chairman Safe. Come in, please, over," a voice called over the device.

"This is Chairman Safe," she replied, her voice steady against the chaos.

"We have the passenger list for you, ma'am," the voice said. There was a pause as she found the strength to ask the dreaded question.

"Was my husband on this flight?" she asked.

A long, heart-stopping pause followed her question. Then,

finally, the voice came back, offering the relief she'd been desperate for.

"No, ma'am. Your husband was not on this flight."

"You're sure?" she asked, needing confirmation.

"Yes, ma'am," the voice confirmed. A sigh of relief escaped her lips as she looked out over the ocean, the darkness of the night mirroring her thoughts.

Meanwhile, the scene was chaotic at the Navy Hospital emergency entrance. Camera crews and frantic family members added to the tumult as medics hustled back and forth, ferrying in patient after patient. A TV crew was setting up for a broadcast.

"Tonight, a Paragon 737 crashed while trying to land at San Diego's Lindbergh Field," the on-camera reporter solemnly reported. "The cause of the crash is unknown at this time, but informed sources speculate it may have been wind shear. Over two hundred passengers were aboard in what may be one of the worst air disasters in US history."

Angry family members crowded in behind the announcer. "Anxious families are gathered here at the navy hospital as the victims are brought in, waiting to find out if their loved ones survived this flight. Tanya Tamara. Channel 11 News."

Imani made her way to the emergency desk amid the chaos. Around her, nurses were swamped with paperwork and the constant influx of information.

"Captain Finicky, what room is he in?" she asked a nurse at the desk.

"Sorry, I can only give that information to the immediate family," the nurse replied apologetically.

Before Imani could respond, an older woman, worry etched on her face, stepped up to the desk.

"I am his wife. What room is my husband in?" she asked, her voice trembling with anxiety. Mrs. Finicky presented her driver's license to the nurse, who quickly scribbled down the room number. As Mrs. Finicky took the slip of paper and went down the crowded hospital corridor, Imani followed silently behind her, the echoes of the night's disaster still ringing in her ears.

The hospital corridor was a flurry of activity, with doctors, nurses, and patients crammed into the equipment-filled space. Amidst this controlled tumult, Mrs. Finicky and Imani rushed along; their steps hurried as they navigated. Mrs. Finicky glanced at the room number on the slip of paper, her face a mixture of worry and determination.

Fraser appeared as they approached the room, closing the door just in time to greet them. "Mrs. Finicky, I'm so sorry this happened," he offered, his tone seemingly sincere.

The look of hate she returned was venomous. "You planned this all along," she accused, her voice icy. Ignoring Fraser's response, she pushed past him and disappeared into the room.

Fraser turned to Imani, his expression recovering quickly from Mrs. Finicky's hostility. "See, you made it to the end zone," he remarked.

"How is he?" Imani asked, ignoring his attempt at humor.

"Oh, he'll play another season," Fraser replied nonchalantly.

"At least the survivor count is going up," Imani added, her voice laced with relief.

"We could use more fans," Fraser retorted, the slight grin on his face widening. His following words, however, stung. "But then, so is the deceased."

"It's awful," said Imani.

"You win some. You lose some," he shrugged, his nonchalant response making her blood boil.

"Is everything a game to you, Fraser?" Imani snapped, her patience wearing thin.

His answer was a wicked smile. "A game of love."

Imani tried to change the subject. "Word has it that you're doing everything possible to keep a lid on this."

"Ugly rumors. See how quickly they spread."

He leaned against the wall with one arm. Then he held her arm and kissed her. She fought to push him away. Despite his age, Fraser was strong. He let go only when she shoved him back.

"What are you doing? Have you gone crazy or something?" Imani asked, her face flushed with anger and embarrassment.

"Crazy for you," he declared, much to her disgust.

Despite her storming off, Fraser wasn't finished. He called after her, his voice loud enough for everyone to hear, making crude comments about their supposed romantic entanglement. His actions were so audacious that even a patient on a stretcher Fraser pointed to was left wide-eyed. Imani quickly disappeared into the crowd, eager to escape his disturbing boyish antics.

Imani fought to exit through the crowd at the Navy hospital emergency entrance with Fraser hot on her heels. "Imani, don't leave me like this. Not again," he pleaded, his voice lacking any sincerity. He caught up with her, grabbing her by the arm.

"What's the big hurry?" he asked, feigning ignorance.

"The big hurry is getting away from you," she replied tersely and yanked free.

Their exchange escalated quickly, with Imani criticizing his flamboyant and arrogant behavior.

"Why? I'm a nice guy," he said.

"Look, if you're trying to humiliate me, you're doing a pretty good job."

"Why would I want to do that?"

"Because that's your style, Fraser." Passersby were gawking at them.

"My style?" he winced.

"Yes, you're an exhibitionist, a megalomaniac, conceited, arrogant, a jerk."

Fraser feigned shock. "No."

When a TV crew began closing in on them, Fraser switched his demeanor, pulling Imani closer and flashing a broad smile for the cameras.

"Smile for the camera, honey," he said, but she wasn't having any of it. She pulled away and left him standing alone in the spotlight's glare.

As Fraser turned to the camera, his face suddenly became somber. He looked every bit the corporate executive, his grief over the tragedy seemingly genuine. The TV crew swooped in, eager for a statement.

"Mr. Gillingham, is it true that the NTSB has already begun their investigation into this tragedy?" the on-camera reporter asked.

"I hope so," Fraser replied, his voice heavy.

"And when will we know who was on this flight?"

"Just as soon as we contact the next of kin and the bodies have been identified. Our deepest sympathies are with the families. Excuse me." He moved away from the camera, leaving the reporter to wrap up the segment.

"There you have it. The heartfelt words from the airline president himself, Fraser Gillingham."

10

Outside the navy hospital, the night sky opened up, unleashing a heavy downpour. Amidst the rain, Imani flagged down a cab. As the vehicle pulled up, she reached for the door handle, but Fraser interjected, stopping her in her tracks.

"I'm sorry. I didn't mean to embarrass you back there. I just got carried away. Can I buy you a drink?" he said, his voice hinting at remorse. She eyed him momentarily, realizing she could not get rid of him, before nodding in agreement.

The atmosphere was considerably more relaxed in the Del Coronado Hotel bar, where they sat nursing their second drink.

"I suppose you think this will allow us to work together?" Imani asked, breaking the silence.

"Absolutely," he replied, his eyes never leaving hers.

"You seem worried," she observed.

"No, just thinking," he corrected her, his gaze still fixed on her.

"About what?"

"This is a terrible thing," he acknowledged.

"It was an accident," she affirmed, her voice heavy with the weight of the tragedy.

"Yeah, maybe," he agreed half-heartedly.

"You don't suspect sabotage, do you?" she asked, surprise coloring her voice.

"No. But you can't rule anything out," he admitted.

"And what concerns you the most?"

"The Board of Directors. I'm going to look like a real jerk explaining how our ninety million dollar jet just fell out of the sky," he confessed, the seriousness of his tone not lost on Imani.

"That's why I'm here," she reassured him, hoping her words would comfort him.

Yet, his mind was already somewhere else. "Stock will drop thirty points as soon as the market opens," he muttered, seemingly more to himself than to her.

"You're not thinking about the families, are you?" she asked, disappointment tingeing her voice.

Fraser leaned in, his voice barely above a whisper as if mentioning money required hushed tones.

"That's my biggest headache. Do you realize that in the Japan crash, the average settlement was $435,000? If the body count keeps going up, we could be looking at close to a hundred million, minimum." He polished off his drink. "If only it had been an international flight. We could have capped each one at seventy-five Gs. I don't know why we didn't push harder for the Montreal Protocols on the domestics."

"Is that all you're thinking about? What is it going to cost you to get out of this?" Imani asked, her voice shaded with disbelief.

He shrugged. "Not exactly. I was hoping I could lay some of it off on Boeing or Pratt & Whitney for bad parts."

"We shouldn't be talking about this. You'll probably ask the Administration not to fine you," she countered.

"You're the one who brought up money. I try to keep the fares down, but if I have to pay you, the government, and the families and pick up your bar tab. Something's got to give," Fraser defended himself.

"And the passengers who died? What about the families who have to live with that, and what about the ones who are maimed? Money won't buy them back," she shot back, her voice filled with anger.

"They could have walked if they weren't in such a hurry. I didn't tell them to fly," he retorted, a spark of defiance in his eyes.

Imani looked at him, stunned. "You haven't changed one bit?"

"I'm a businessman. Reciting Buddhist sutras for the families of the dead isn't going to bring them any comfort," he stated bluntly, sipping his drink in a last act of defiance. Imani stood, shook her head, and headed to the lobby.

Imani approached the registration desk inside the hotel, catching the desk clerk's attention.

"Do I have any messages?" she asked, a hint of hope in her voice.

The clerk checked her box, only to find it empty. "No, Mrs. Safe. I'll call you if we hear anything."

She nodded and slowly headed back to the bar, where fresh drinks awaited her on the table. Fraser was still there, seemingly deep in thought. Finally, she rejoined him.

"This will take days to clean up," Fraser said.

"Maybe weeks."

She looked at him as though he was a pathetic specimen or a relic from the past.

"You never married, did you?" she asked, breaking the silence.

"You can tell?" he responded with a small smile.

"Plainly. Why not?" she pressed, curiosity glinting in her eyes.

He sipped his drink before replying, "I tried it once. Living together, but you know, the minute I looked at another girl, I could see the handcuffs coming out. I don't need a ring to confirm that kind of sentence."

"So you never had children, either?" she queried, her gaze fixed on him.

He shrugged, a hint of mischief playing on his lips. "Oh, there might be a couple of little bastards running around. But no one ever told me."

She raised an eyebrow at his statement, her interest piqued. "So, you wouldn't miss them?"

He met her gaze with a soulful stare. "Imani, do I look like the kind of guy who'd make a good father?"

"You were the one we all thought would be the first. Get married. Settle down," she reminisced, a touch of nostalgia in her voice.

He smirked. "You want to know the truth?"

"Of course. Although every time you preface with that, I think you're getting ready to lie," she quipped, eyeing him with a painful smile.

He leaned in, his eyes flickering. "Then here's the big lie."

"Yes?" She shrugged, pretending innocence.

"I fooled around with a lot of units," he confessed.

"Units?" she asked, a little taken aback by his choice of words.

He sighed, his gaze never leaving hers. "But I never tied the knot because, after you, I never felt like I found the right girl."

"Except me?" she asked, her voice barely a whisper.

"Except you, my high school sweetheart. But that was tricky," he replied, a tender smile spreading across his face.

"That was twenty-two years ago," she retorted, trying to hide the tremor in her voice.

"Seems like yesterday," he mused, his eyes clouded with nostalgia.

"In all that time, you never once met a woman you could live with and care for? Not even a White girl?" she challenged, her gaze steady on him.

"I told you you wouldn't believe me," he said, shrugging.

"Where have you been looking? They're everywhere. They're at the market. They're at the office," she asserted, trying to reason with him.

"They must be invisible because the only one I see is you, and you're the only girl I could ever marry," he declared, his gaze filled with sincerity.

She stiffened, taken aback by his statement. "You missed your chance."

"Geez, I've been kicking myself ever since," he admitted, his expression one of regret.

11

Fraser escorted Imani to her room in the peaceful silence of the hotel corridor. The suggestion of a question hung in the air between them.

"You sure you don't want to come in for a nightcap? My room is right down the hall," he asked, his tone hopeful.

"You're asking the wrong girl, Fraser," Imani replied, her voice firm.

"For old times' sake?" Fraser pressed, a nostalgic smile playing on his lips.

"I don't remember that in the old times," she retorted, putting a definitive end to his attempts. He responded by planting a chaste kiss on her cheek and making a playful attempt to grab her behind, only to have his hand stopped by hers. He moved away, allowing her the space to unlock her door. Suddenly, Fraser stopped short.

"Oh, I almost forgot. I had the San Francisco crew pull a *revised* manifest for you. A flight attendant confirmed it," he stated casually.

"Confirmed what?" she asked, turning to face him.

"Your husband, Orville. He *was* on the flight. It's a shame," Fraser revealed, his eyes avoiding hers.

Imani froze at his words, shock etched on her face. "You bastard. You knew all along. Why didn't you say something?" she questioned, her voice laced with betrayal.

Avoiding eye contact, Fraser merely shrugged and shuffled his feet. "Thought I could get a little piece of ass for old time's sake," he justified.

Outraged, Imani stormed into her room and slammed the door behind her.

Once inside, she turned on a light and went to the window. From her high vantage point, she looked out over the stillness of the night.

Back in the hotel corridor, Fraser stood outside Imani's door, his hands tucked in his pockets. He was about to knock but thought better of it and retreated.

In her room, Imani remained unmoving, her gaze fixed on the darkened sea. Abruptly, she spun around, a determined look in her eyes.

She raced along the empty white deck of the hotel, the foggy night enveloping her. Imani moved swiftly down a set of stairs that led to the beach.

On the beach, the wind whipped through her hair as she ran along the surf's edge, the dense fog swallowing her silhouette. She kept going, her pace never faltering, her footprints disappearing behind her in the sand. Her figure became increasingly distant until it finally dissolved into the foggy night.

·   ·   ·

As the first blush of daybreak painted the sky, Imani found herself on the beach; her gaze lost in the vast expanse of the Pacific. The tide brought bits and pieces of crash debris, turning the once tranquil seascape into a grim reminder of the disaster. The distant hum of a lifeguard truck cut through the silence, drawing closer to where she stood.

In the dawn's stillness, a man's voice rang out from the sea, weak and exhausted. The voice belonged to a survivor, clinging onto hope and life amidst the sea's vast indifference.

"Help. Over here," he called out, his voice trembling with fatigue and relief.

"Where are you?" Imani called back, her eyes scanning through the coastal fog for any signs of the survivor.

"Here. I'm right here," came the response, desperation clear in his voice.

Imani flagged down the Lifeguard as the truck approached. "There's a man out there," she alerted him, pointing out to sea.

Without wasting a moment, the Lifeguard snatched a life preserver from the truck and charged into the surf. Imani followed close on his heels, her heart pounding in her chest.

"Right here. I'm alive. I can't believe it. I'm alive," the survivor laughed, his hysteria echoing off the waves.

"Here, grab onto this," the Lifeguard instructed, throwing him a line. Through the early morning fog, they caught sight of the man, buoyant and clinging to a fragment of the inflatable slide.

"I can't move my arms. They must be frozen or something," the man confessed, his voice barely audible over the crashing waves.

The Lifeguard plunged into the surf, securing the man and towing him back towards the beach. A brief exchange ensued before the Lifeguard tied the man and the slide off, coiling enough rope to secure them to a rock on the shore.

"You can't just leave him out there," Imani protested, her eyes wide with disbelief.

"He needs medical attention. Looks like his back is broken," the Lifeguard explained, his voice steady despite the gravity of the situation.

"But the sharks'll get him," she countered, a sick dread settling in her stomach.

"They already have," the Lifeguard declared, the reality of his words hanging heavy in the air. "I don't think you want to be around for this."

12

———————

Later that day, back at the hotel, the desk clerk flagged down Imani as she entered the lobby. The hope in her eyes quickly dissipated as he shook his head, signaling there was still no word.

Imani walked from room to room in the hospital, looking for Orville. Desperation tugged at her heart, each second stretching into eternity.

Imani hurried into the bustling hospital cafeteria, her gaze sweeping across the patients and the hospital staff.

Then, amidst the sea of unfamiliar faces, she spotted her husband. A nurse was pushing Orville in a wheelchair. The breakfast choice was bacon, eggs, and juice, which the nurse placed onto Orville's tray before they moved toward the cash register. A surge of relief washed over Imani as she rushed towards him.

"Orville?" Her voice trembled with anticipation and relief. As she recognized him, she threw her arms around his neck, tears of joy in her eyes. His wince of pain was instant.

"Ow ow," he protested, trying to ease out of her embrace.

"Are you all right? I'm so happy to see you," Imani gushed, gently kissing his forehead.

"My neck. I have a fractured clavicle," Orville informed her, managing a faint smile.

"If that's all that's wrong?" Imani asked, her voice barely a whisper. She noticed a blanket covering his legs, and her heart sank.

"No, there's something else," he replied.

With hesitant hands, she lifted the cover and went white as she saw one of Orville's legs encased in a walking cast.

"Damn fool doctors, it took me two hours to convince them they cast the wrong leg. I should know. I'm the one who has to walk on it," Orville grumbled, struggling to stand. He shoved the wheelchair away with a grimace. "Just give me the crutches. I don't need this thing. Use it for someone who really can't walk. I meant to call, but..."

The nurse hurriedly collected the wheelchair, but Imani quickly reassured him, "It's okay. I've got him."

With newfound strength, she supported Orville, carrying his tray to a nearby table where they sat.

"You're the best damn thing I've seen all morning," she said, her voice brimming with adoration.

"Want some breakfast, lady?" Orville asked, offering a lopsided grin.

"I want you," Imani replied sincerely, leaning across the table to kiss his lips tenderly.

"Don't suppose you'd care for seconds?" Orville asked, his eyes twinkling with mischief.

"And thirds and fourths," Imani shot back, her laughter echoing around the cafeteria.

"I knew I made a mistake by using your name to get on that flight," Orville confessed, his voice choked with emotion.

Another loving kiss from Imani was his reward. "Except for this broken leg, I guess it wasn't a mistake after all."

"Oh, my God. I'm so relieved. I love you," Imani whispered, her eyes shimmering with unshed tears.

"Feeling's mutual, lady," Orville replied, pulling her into a hug. Their embrace was warm, and comforting, a testament to their enduring love, a hug that felt like it could go on forever.

Later, Imani and Orville stepped into a brightly lit, cavernous hangar. Scattered tables and chairs were huddled at one end, creating the illusion of an impromptu workspace.

"Your new office?" Orville inquired, his eyes scanning the expansive hangar.

"I'll use it for a few days," Imani replied, already visualizing her temporary workspace.

"Guess that means you're staying?"

"I have to. I have staff coming in," she clarified, watching as Orville eased himself into a chair.

"Well, what are we waiting for? Turn your tape recorder on."

"You don't have to do this," Imani interjected, her eyes softening with concern.

"Don't you want to hear how I floated into Mission Bay doing the backstroke? I avoided the sharks," Orville joked, though the humor didn't quite reach his eyes.

"Not right now," she answered quietly.

"Or what about how that inboard spoiler stayed up when the floor ripped apart?" he continued, oblivious to her growing unease.

"No. I'm just glad you're here. I don't want to hear about all the ways I could have lost you," Imani admitted, her voice barely a whisper.

"Kids'll be glad to see us," Orville said, changing the topic abruptly. He got up, using one crutch as a makeshift golf club, taking a playful swing.

"Oh, I forgot to tell you. Darius has measles," she shared her gaze, following his mock golf swing.

Fraser Gillingham's entrance interrupted their conversation.

"Hope I'm not disturbing anything?" he asked, stepping further into the hangar.

"No, come on in, Fraser. You remember my husband, Orville? Fraser Gillingham, president of the infamous airline," Imani introduced, her tone laced with a hint of sarcasm.

"I wouldn't say that too loudly around here. Liable to get me in trouble," Fraser quipped, shaking Orville's hand.

"Yes, how are you? It's been a long time," Orville greeted him.

"I just came by to tell you that the crew recovered the black box in one piece. Thought you might want to know," Fraser relayed before departing.

Later, Imani clung to Orville at the departure level of the airport, their goodbye hug lingering.

"I'll take care of the kids." He assured her.

"I know you will. You always do. Thank you."

With a last wave, he ascended the escalator and disappeared from sight.

In the hangar's emptiness, the flight deck voice recorder tape spun in a cassette, filling the silent expanse with echoes of past voices. The cacophony of radio clicks and engine noise interfered with the conversation, and some responses were garbled or spoken too quickly to decipher.

"Can I see that map?" The flight engineer's voice filtered through the noise.

The copilot responded, "We want to stay offshore, then just come in by the Del Mar racetrack."

"You got that traffic?" Finicky's voice asked.

"We got him, but we lost him for a second."

"Where's the DC10?" The pilot's voice asked, concern tingeing his words.

"He's long gone. It's the Mooney that's screwing me up," the copilot answered, his voice strained.

"I see him," said the engineer.

Finicky's voice reported. "Traffic in sight. Down to seven five heading zero eight zero. Paragon 860."

Imani, Fraser, Lester, and a group of FAA, airline, and National Transportation Safety Board staff gathered around the table, all eyes on the playback. Suddenly, a loud thud echoed over the jet engines.

"What was that?" Finicky's voice came through, filled with alarm.

The copilot's voice crackled through the recorder. "A bird?"

"Sounded like a car door," the flight engineer speculated.

13

"Piper triple eight RJ San Diego Departure radar contact, maintain VFR conditions at or below 3,500. Fly heading 070, vector final approach course," the controller's voice relayed instructions, disembodied, flat, and procedural.

"Zero seven zero on the heading. VFR below thirty-five. Triple eight RJ," a Piper pilot's voice confirmed the instructions.

Imani signaled the technician. "Skip ahead," she commanded.

"We'll be able to clean it up for you," the technician promised, fingers hovering over the controls.

"No, I want it like this," she responded, focusing on the spinning tape. The technician fast-forwarded the tape, and at her nod, he halted the playback.

"Okay, sir, maintain visual separation. Contact Tower 118.3. Have a nice day now," the approach control's voice continued, only to be abruptly cut off by the shriek of a stall warning.

"Easy baby, easy baby. Get the nose down," the flight engineer's voice urged, desperation creeping into his voice.

"We're breaking up. We're hit, man. We're hit," the copilot's voice echoed, full of fear and panic.

Fraser shut off the tape, the sudden silence in the hangar deafening. "Pretty clear, isn't it?" he asked, looking at Imani.

"We'll look at the transcript," she replied, her voice steady.

"I thought these problems were behind us," Fraser muttered, running a hand through his hair.

"We'll review the transcript," she reiterated.

"We can't be putting ninety million dollar jets in the air if we still have incompetent greenhorns in the tower," Fraser exploded, anger flashing in his eyes.

"I said we will review the full record, Mr. Gillingham," Imani countered, maintaining her calm.

"Who are you kidding, Chairman? That flight was an instrument approach controlled from the tower, *your* tower, guided by *your* staff, and he's got some little Piper tooting around up there in marginal VFR, and the goddamned controller tells him to maintain visual separation? He never even called the Piper traffic to my flight. Did you hear that? Never."

"Are you through?" She asked.

"Momentarily." He huffed.

"There may have been other aircraft in the vicinity, but if the controller considered it significant, he would have advised the flight."

Fraser raged on, stepping closer to Imani until their noses almost touched. "How close does a plane have to be to be significant, Chairman? This close? Or this close?" He illustrated his point by pulling away and then moving closer again.

"If another plane was a factor, there's no evidence of it yet. We have no missing small planes. They found no other wreck-age," Imani replied, holding her ground.

"Not yet," Fraser snarled, spinning away in frustration.

"You think there was another aircraft?" Imani asked, watching his retreating figure.

"Damn right there was, and I'm going to find it if I have to drag the ocean floor myself," Fraser declared.

"Do you have anything else to say before we begin the formal investigation, Mr. Gillingham?" Imani asked, redirecting the conversation back to the matter at hand.

"No," Fraser's answer was curt.

"We can expect the airline's full cooperation?" Imani pressed, needing assurance.

"Have I ever refused you before, Madam Chairman?" Fraser countered, a bitter smile twisting his lips. "Oh, I do have one final question."

"Yes?" she asked.

"What kind of perfume are you wearing? Seduction?"

Under the blistering sun, Fraser caressed the red cloth covers on his Lear's Pitot tubes. The airport apron buzzed with noise, but Fraser was in his own world until Imani arrived, disturbing his serenity.

"You mind telling me what got into you back there?" she demanded, her voice slicing through the ambient noise.

Fraser's hand moved over the plane's sleek nose as he responded, "She's a beauty, isn't she?"

"Are you listening to me?" Imani's voice rose in frustration. "I'm trying to conduct an investigation, and you're turning it into a three-ring circus."

"I didn't bring in any elephants or fire-eaters, but you sure brought in the clowns," Fraser shot back, his gaze not leaving the aircraft.

"Those people belong here," Imani argued, crossing her arms.

"Imani, I already got the press, the insurance investigators, and the Board of Directors breathing down my neck because the stockholders are breathing down theirs," Fraser explained, his voice curt. "I don't need the NTSB and every other government agency sticking their nose into this and blowing smoke up my ass. I just want to keep it a real clean, low-key thing, just between you and me."

"Why?" she pressed.

"It's easier that way, and it won't cost the taxpayers as much money," Fraser rationalized.

"In case you've forgotten why I'm here. I am the NTSB. It is my duty to investigate this accident properly," she pointed out sternly.

"Screw your duty," Fraser muttered.

"If I don't do that, then I shouldn't be running this agency," Imani said firmly.

Fraser mocked her, mimicking in a high-pitched voice, "'Oh, teachers going to make you stay after school and write that a hundred times on the board. I shouldn't be running this agency, I shouldn't be running this agency.'"

"It's my job," she retorted.

"Fine. Let's not blow it out of proportion, okay?" Fraser suggested.

"People were killed on your plane, Fraser. One hundred and eighty-one dead. Within a few minutes. So don't tell me not to blow this thing out of proportion," Imani fired back, her eyes flashing angrily.

"All I'm saying is do it the right way. That's all I'm saying," Fraser insisted.

"Don't tell me how to do my job," Imani spat, storming off, only to halt and spin around. "What do you mean, 'do it the right way?'"

"Your predecessor wouldn't have been so zealous," Fraser stated smugly.

"And that's why I'm here, and he's not," she countered, anger still burning in her voice.

"I told the President he was making a mistake by appointing you," Fraser confessed.

"Thanks a lot. Do I go to your boss and tell him you're no good for the airline?" Imani retorted sarcastically.

"No, but it has been tried before," Fraser chuckled.

"Fraser, look, don't make this any more difficult than it has to be," Imani pleaded, frustration lining her voice.

"I just want the whole thing to blow over, Imani. Just like you do, put all the players to bed, so to speak," Fraser said with a slight smile.

"Well, you're not getting this player into bed," Imani retorted grimly.

"Investigators get very lonely at night, Imani. Burning the midnight oil listening to all those terrible stories over and over again," Fraser continued to tease.

"I'll manage," she snapped, exasperated.

Fraser leaned against his Lear as Imani walked off, shouting after her. "Great having you back again. Maybe we'll go flying?"

"No," she yelled back, her voice becoming distant.

"I can perform some pretty fantastic maneuvers midair," he laughed.

"Perform them on yourself," she shot back before disappearing inside the hangar.

Fraser found himself alone, chuckling to himself. "Jesus, I like a woman with spunk."

14

In the massive hangar, Imani was surrounded by a fortress of photographs and documents. The air was stale, with the smell of old paper and dust. Lester shattered the silence as he arrived with a large brown envelope, multiple tapes, and a pot of hot coffee.

"You're working late," he observed, his eyes scanning the paper labyrinth surrounding her. I thought you could use this. It's black, right?" He gestured towards the pot of coffee in his hands.

Imani nodded in gratitude as he filled a cup for her.

"These are the control tower tapes. Transcripts are being typed up now. They'll be ready in the morning," Lester explained.

Her attention shifted to the large brown envelope bearing the Paragon Airlines company label. "What's that?" Imani inquired, her voice reverberating in the expansive hangar.

"It's Paragon's accident report," he said, handing her the envelope.

Imani's fingers tore open the envelope, pulling out a meager single-paged report. Her eyes scanned the document. "This is it?" She couldn't help but voice her surprise. "One page? He's got to be kidding."

Lester shrugged in response.

"Lester, I want a complete list of the flight crew. I want toxicology reports and background information on everyone associated with that flight," she demanded, her voice echoing through the hangar.

"Ground crew, too?" Lester asked, his voice uncertain.

"Ground crew, drivers, handlers, ticket agents. Everyone. I want the schedules for everyone working that day and the flight crew for the past month," she ordered, her voice stern and unwavering.

"Do you know what you're asking for?" Lester questioned, his hand poised over a notepad.

"And I'll need the maintenance schedules, work orders, invoices, canceled checks, and Boeing's specs, revisions, and recommendations for maintenance of that plane," she continued, unfazed by his question.

Lester's pen raced across the page, trying to keep up with her rapid-fire requests. "Slow down," he protested.

"I want five direct lines to Washington and a tie-in to the data bank," she persisted, her eyes locked on him.

"Five?" he questioned, his eyebrows raised in surprise.

"Five. I need a forensic team. Also, I want the best statistical analysts we've got. They need to develop a direct simulation of all airport traffic over the last seventy-two hours," she elaborated, her gaze now fixed on the sea of documents before her.

"Seventy-two hours?" Lester echoed, looking incredulous.

"Better yet, make it a compressed distribution over the last three months. Include all meteorological and atmospheric effects within a fifty-mile radius of the airport. I want the legal firm Silver, Cohen, Harbinger, and Dheume to render an opinion on this and to monitor all our proceedings independently," she further instructed.

"Anything else?" Lester asked, his voice filled with a mix of disbelief and awe.

"Just one. I'll need Paragon's financial statements for the last five years and Wall Street's opinion of them compared to the other airlines and the industry as a whole. When you're done with that, I'd like more coffee," she replied with a faint smile.

"I suppose you want all of this tonight," Lester mused, his tone laced with apprehension.

"First thing in the morning would be fine," she retorted, returning to her mountain of paperwork. The hangar was silent, save for the rustle of papers and the occasional pen scribble.

The next day, inside the bustling hangar, phone installers and computer technicians skittered around, cabling in terminals, modems, and phone lines. Teams from the manufacturer, the insurance company, and the NTSB pressed in. A moving crew rolled in, setting up several more desks amidst the chaos.

"Are these okay here?" one of the movers asked, gesturing towards the newly installed desks.

"Fine," Imani responded, her eyes scanning the rapidly expanding workspace. The hum of printers filled the air, and phones rang incessantly.

"Computers ready to go," a technician declared. A secretary approached Imani, a stack of paperwork in her hands.

"I'll have copies of those analysts' reports by noon," she informed her.

"Good," Imani replied, nodding in approval.

Amid all this activity, Lester cornered Imani. He cleared his throat, his face flushed. "Listen, I know you know what you're doing, Imani, but don't you think you ought to at least wait for the dust to settle?" he queried, concern etched on his face.

"Lester, I thought you were on my side," Imani countered, her eyebrows knitted together.

"I am, but I didn't think it would get this complex," Lester defended himself, looking somewhat flustered.

"This isn't complex. This is being thorough," Imani retorted, crossing her arms.

"What I mean to say is that by pushing too hard, you could lose credibility," Lester cautioned, trying to make her understand his perspective.

"Credibility with whom?" Imani snapped back, her patience thinning.

"This is a very hot issue right now. You don't want to make anyone mad," Lester warned, his voice barely more than a whisper.

Imani grabbed her coat, shooting him a determined look. "You're wrong. I do."

"It's not going to help," Lester replied, his voice filled with resignation.

"Look, I have to get to the morgue. I'll see if anyone's mad over there," Imani declared, storming out of the bustling hangar.

At the county morgue, the grim atmosphere was a stark contrast to the activity of the hangar. Imani and the chief coroner watched as an assistant pulled a cloth-covered body from the vault. An elderly couple watched with them, the woman breaking down as the sheet was lifted, exposing what remained of a face.

The husband handed a file to the coroner. "The dental records?" the coroner inquired, glancing at the woman.

"And my son's fingerprints," she replied through her tears.

The coroner examined the documents, comparing them to

another file. "They match. If you could sign right here," he instructed, showing them the paperwork.

The woman, overwhelmed with grief, fell apart. She clutched at Imani's collar, her eyes filled with a desperate plea. "Who did this to him? He was a fine boy. He was going to be a doctor. How could they do this to my son? How could they murder him like this?"

Her husband tried to pull her away, but she wouldn't let go of Imani. "You'll help us, won't you? You'll find out who did this and make sure this doesn't happen again?" she pleaded, her voice filled with sorrow and desperation.

15

I n the somber cemetery, grieving families convened for multiple burial ceremonies. Imani looked around, searching for a particular face in the crowd. Fraser was notably absent

A colossal crane hauled up a large section of the plane in a vast field by a nearby tidepool, loading it onto a flatbed tractor-trailer. Rescuers, their hands encased in rubber gloves and faces obscured by alcohol-soaked masks, scrambled to recover more charred remains.

"It really stinks," a rescuer muttered, his voice muffled.

"What do you expect?" the truck driver responded, his expression impassive.

Further along, NTSB examiners worked alongside rescue teams. Every scrap on the field was gathered, tagged, and tossed into marked boxes. They sprinkled meat preserver over the scattered body parts as latex-gloved hands collected them meticulously. A trail of debris crossed a fence, and the men hopped over it with ease.

In a suburban street, a group of children bounced up and down on a section of airline seats on their front lawn. An NTSB investigator activated his walkie-talkie. "This is field team two. We need the pickup," he reported.

"You taking this?" a kid asked, eyeing the investigator curiously.

"Yeah," he confirmed.

A piece of the empennage lay at the curb. The crew moved in to collect it. An older adult was mowing his lawn nearby, observing the scene with bemusement. "Another one, huh?" he asked, pausing his task.

"Yeah," the investigator replied, focusing on the task.

"Strangest things fall from the sky," the old man mused, resuming his mowing. Soon after, the pickup truck arrived at the scene.

At sea, a rescue boat with a hydraulic slewing arm crane bobbed on the waves. A steel cable rose through the pounding surf. A heavyset rigger watched the operation intently. "Easy now. Easy now," he cautioned.

Two scuba divers emerged from the water. The cable hoisted a small damaged plane out of the water a moment later. On the boat, Fraser smiled a satisfied smile.

Fraser and Imani walked through a hangar with damaged plane parts and crash evidence.

"Any conclusions so far?" Fraser asked, his gaze fixed on Imani.

"Just observations," she replied, her expression focused.

He reached inside his jacket pocket and retrieved a document. He handed it to her. "If it's not interfering too much, I tracked down the pilot of that Piper Triple Eight RJ," he informed her.

"He survived?" Imani asked, surprise coloring her tone.

"Oh, he wasn't hit," Fraser revealed with a trace of relief in his voice.

"So, he wasn't a factor, after all?" Imani questioned, eyes scanning Fraser's face for hints of withheld information.

"Just read what it says," Fraser suggested, an enigmatic smile on his lips.

Imani's eyes moved down to the document, absorbing the contents rapidly. "You must be happy," she declared, mildly sarcastic.

"He saw the second plane in CAVU conditions. Clear and visibility unlimited, in case you've forgotten what that means," Fraser teased her lightly.

"I know what it means," she retorted, irritation creeping into her voice.

"And he saw it just a few minutes before the plane went down."

Her brows furrowed. "Why didn't he come forward before?"

"He had his reasons," Fraser responded cryptically. He reached out and laid a comforting arm around her, but Imani stepped back, subtly evading the contact.

"Look, I know this comes as a blow to you just when you're trying to get these Terminal Control Areas cleaned up. You don't need a problem like this right now," Fraser stated, his tone empathetic.

"What are you getting at?" Imani asked warily, her eyes narrowing in suspicion.

"Well, a couple of close friends in the business. We're going down to Acapulco for the weekend. Get in a little sun, a little golf. You still play?" Fraser queried, changing the subject with finesse.

"Rarely," Imani replied, her brows knitted in thought.

"Why don't you take time off? Let these guys do their work. We'd love to have you join us. Give you a chance to reflect on what's happened here. What do you say?" Fraser proposed, his voice filled with genuine concern and smooth persuasion.

"I'll let you know," Imani responded noncommittally, not entirely buying into Fraser's idea.

"Look, even if you want to come down for a half-day or something, that'd be fine. You don't have to stay the whole time," Fraser added, hoping to sway her decision.

16

Later in the hangar, Imani's staff and all the investigators assembled around a table, surrounded by the tangible evidence of their work: reports, photographs, interviews, simulations, and analyses.

"Well, Gillingham was right about that other plane. They dragged it up today. Nobody had it on the radar anywhere," the photographer noted, peering at the others from behind a stack of photos.

"We haven't received all the interviews yet, but it looks like the flight crew was clean and sober, and they had all their shots," the secretary interjected, shuffling through a stack of paper.

"Tower, Departure, and Approach tapes all tie to the flight deck activity. Looks like everyone was heads up," Lester added, his voice thoughtful.

Imani turned to the remainder of the team, focusing her gaze on one of them. "Jim?" she prompted.

"Maintenance records showed that all required work had been performed on the plane before liftoff. She was a bit old, but the operations she's had were successful," the researcher responded, his gaze firmly on the notes in front of him.

"Operations?" Imani asked, her brow furrowing in confusion.

"In '83, Paragon had problems with a series of Pratt and Whitney engines on their DC-10s. Still, the Boeing fan on the 737 was solid, and it looked like they maintained it after they spent a hundred thou replacing them the first time," Jim elaborated.

"What about the broken blade I saw?" Imani questioned, her tone grave.

"Looks like it happened as a result of the crash. We found a seagull in the left engine pod, or part of one anyway. The seagull was small enough to get through, so we suspect it got hit first and then got sucked in. The rest of the damaged blade happened when the plane came to rest after hitting a rock in the ground," Jim replied.

"And the path of that cut behind the rear spoiler to the tail?" Imani queried, her mind busily piecing together the information.

"The fan definitely traveled aft, but I don't think it could slice through the cabin like that. That makes the mystery plane the likely target and would indicate a traffic problem since he was hit just inside the TCA," Jim mused.

"They were eighteen miles out," Imani countered.

"But the impact was a few minutes later," the researcher corrected.

It made little sense to her. But she pressed on. "What about their past record? I remember something in Washington," Imani asked.

"September 5th. A DC-10 returned to Dulles right after takeoff with control problems. A nut holding part of the stabilizer had vibrated loose."

"Three days later, another DC-10 rolled into a mobile

lounge at the same airport and pushed it into a neighboring jet, according to the analyst," Imani filled in.

"For 1985..." the secretary began.

"Interrupting her, Imani noted, "The worst year in aviation history."

"Yes, all the airlines reported a total of 617 incidents, from birds to loose parts, onboard fires to strange noises to near misses. Paragon didn't incur a more significant share of anything than anyone else, except maybe some of the smaller carriers and the privates," the secretary added.

"We were still recovering from the machinists' strike in '85," Imani commented.

"That's right," Jim agreed.

"I thought there were a lot of disgruntled mechanics?" Imani pondered aloud.

"There were," he confirmed.

"Don't you think it's odd that the mechanics were unhappy yet worked on the planes as diligently as before?" Imani questioned, an edge to her voice.

"You don't want to scare the flying public. They'd get real nervous about flying. Where would we be then?" Lester responded, lightening the heavy atmosphere with a bit of humor. A smattering of chuckles filled the room.

"What have you got on the financials, Sandy?" Imani asked, turning her attention to a middle-aged woman with glasses perched on the bridge of her nose.

"Earnings have remained consistent for the past five years, thanks to stable fuel costs and internal reorganization, despite some write-downs of depreciable assets. Despite industry problems, they've been able to grow," Sandy explained, her fingers tapping a rhythm on a thick report.

"Even with the low fare discounting?" Imani challenged, leaning back in her chair.

"They run an eighty-nine percent load factor, and their

revenue passenger miles keep going up, Chairman. Wall Street says they've got real clean trend lines for a carrier," Sandy confidently answered.

"Real clean trend lines?" Imani echoed, her brow furrowed in thought.

"That's right—smooth growth. Managed very well, it looks like," Sandy confirmed, her tone resolute.

"Expenses down?" Imani probed, her gaze scrutinizing Sandy.

"Substantially," Sandy replied, nodding for emphasis.

"Smoothly, of course?" Imani asked, a hint of skepticism lacing her words.

"I wasn't looking that closely," Sandy admitted, a flush creeping up her cheeks.

"Can you tell me how, with stiff competition in this industry, management salaries and union salaries would go up, the cost of new planes kept rising, and yet the fares have gone down?" Imani posed her question to the room at large.

"Volume. Better scheduling. Computerization," Jim offered, attempting to fill the uncomfortable silence that had settled.

"Is that true?" Imani turned her questioning gaze back to Sandy.

"They picked up a few new routes. Usually, it takes a couple of years to get into the black. They're doing it in months," Sandy confirmed, her voice steadier now.

"Have maintenance costs gone down?" Imani asked, her tone bordering on accusatory.

"Yes, I believe I said that," Sandy responded, slightly taken aback.

"Didn't fire any mechanics?" Imani questioned, her gaze unwavering.

"None to speak of," Jim answered, his voice unsure.

"So, how did they reduce their maintenance expenses?" Imani queried, looking at each member of the team. They all looked back at her, their expressions blank. No one had an answer.

"Chairman, there's nothing that would show a deferred maintenance program was in effect if that's what you're getting at?" Lester attempted to ease the tension, his gaze challenging.

"I'm just puzzled," Imani confessed, her tone thoughtful. "You're telling me we had a reputable airline with a model crew on a routine flight in a plane that never broke down? And they fly into an airport where the controllers, although somewhat inexperienced, handle the day's traffic better than most. Is that right?" she finished, looking around the room.

The group agreed, voicing their assent.

Sandy said, "Yeah." Jim agreed. "No question," the analyst added, "Absolutely right."

"I still have one question, then," Imani posed, her gaze sweeping the room. "If everything was so perfect, why did this plane crash?"

17

I n the hangar, the rumbling sound of a small plane being wheeled through the massive open doors resonated in the cavernous space. Two men maneuvered it with practiced ease while Imani waited alongside an experienced NTSB investigator. The slightly battered but intact plane bore testament to an incident still shrouded in mystery.

"Did the pilot survive?" Imani asked, eyeing the small aircraft critically.

"We don't know. Must have. He wasn't there," the investigator replied, his gaze following Imani's.

"No report?"

"That's right. I ran a check on the R.O. The plane was stolen. A few days ago. The owner claims he didn't know until we informed him," the investigator explained, his eyes never leaving the plane.

"It doesn't look that bad for falling eight thousand feet," Imani commented, her eyebrows furrowing.

"Must have known how to ditch it. Drugs. Who knows?" He shrugged.

"You know, this plane doesn't look like it hit a 737 standing still," Imani noted, her eyes still scanning the aircraft.

"I agree," he said, leading her to the wing's trailing edge by the ailerons, where a large section had ripped out. "The only damage this plane suffered is right here."

"The plane would become unstable, most likely stall, spin, crash, and burn. The usual scenario," Imani mused aloud, her gaze on the torn aileron.

"Right, and if it hit the 737, the pilot had to be flying this thing backward because he ran into the jet with the rear of his wing. That's some pretty fancy flying, wouldn't you say?" he asked, a hint of disbelief in his tone.

Imani didn't reply, instead circling to the nose of the aircraft. "From eight thousand feet, there should be no front end. The plane should have folded in half."

The NTSB investigator smiled at her assessment. "Like a beach chair."

"So either this isn't the mystery plane, or there's a third one we still haven't found," Imani said, her brow furrowing in thought.

"Personally, I'm sticking with the one-plane theory," the investigator responded, folding his arms over his chest.

"Other investigators have jumped to conclusions that way," Imani pointed out, a slight edge to her voice.

"I get the feeling we're staring right at the problem, only we're so close we can't see it," he mused, his gaze still fixed on the plane.

"It's funny. Everything fits so smoothly, and then this?" Imani asked, a trace of frustration creeping into her voice.

"Sloppy work is what I say," he shrugged.

At his words, something clicked in Imani's mind. "What did you say?" she asked, her eyes wide.

"Sloppy work. The guy who did this was getting sloppy," he repeated, unaware of the revelation his words sparked.

Imani raced off without another word, leaving a puzzled investigator behind.

"Where are you going?" he called after her.

"I'll see you at the hearing," Imani said without breaking stride.

18

The hearing commenced with the FAA, the NTSB, airline and manufacturer representatives, the chief coroner, a selection of witnesses, and survivors in attendance. It was like a modified grand jury. No judge, no defense.

As the speaker, Imani exuded confidence, her assertive voice echoing through the room.

"This hearing has been called to provide testimony and new information into the crash of Paragon flight 860. Until now, this incident has baffled the best examiners from the safety board, the insurance company, and the airline," she stated, addressing the roomful of anxious individuals. Fraser, meanwhile, sat coolly, whispering to his team of attorneys.

Imani continued, her tone resolute. "We will present facts that will not only explain the series of events leading to this unfortunate tragedy but will also recommend preventing similar errors from happening again in the NTSB's and FAA's final report. You may proceed, Mr. Harbinger."

Steve Harbinger, a seasoned attorney in a no-nonsense brown suit, steered the questioning of the tower controllers. His firm, Silver, Cohen, Harbinger, and Dheume, was known for its tenacity, a trait he personified in his relentless pursuit of the truth. Imani, Lester, and other important figures were also present, their eyes riveted on the unfolding exchange.

"At the time of the accident, how many hours had you been on?" Harbinger began his voice firm.

"Sixteen," the tower controller replied, his voice filled with the fatigue of a long ordeal.

"Don't the regulations permit only eight, a maximum of twelve in any twenty-four period?" Harbinger pushed, his gaze as intense as his voice.

"Yes, but there were extenuating circumstances," the controller defended, his forehead creased in worry.

"The FARs would put you in violation of 14 CFR Part 117.51," Harbinger pointed out, looking over his notes.

"What am I supposed to do? Get up and leave?" the controller asked, his voice defiant.

"I'm not here to advise you. Just answer the question," Harbinger replied, unyielding.

"We did perform a hand-off when the Chairman commented on my time," he confessed, a hint of unease slipping into his voice.

"You performed a hand-off?" Harbinger repeated, raising an eyebrow.

"Yes, sir," the controller confirmed, his voice barely more than a whisper now.

"When you had heavy inbound traffic, you switched controllers?" Harbinger continued, his words falling heavily in the silent room.

"Yes, sir," he confirmed again, his gaze dropping to his hands.

"And how long did this hand-off take?" Harbinger asked, his gaze still fixed on the man.

"A couple of minutes," he responded, his voice trembling slightly.

"A couple of minutes? What, five, ten, fifteen? An hour?" Harbinger's words sliced through the room's silence, each question hitting the witness like a physical blow.

"No, it didn't take an hour," he defended, his gaze shifting nervously.

"How long did it take?" Harbinger demanded, his patience wearing thin.

"He just took the seat," he finally confessed, his voice barely audible.

At this, Imani closed her eyes and rubbed her forehead, feeling the weight of the situation press down upon her.

"That'll be all. Can we have the next witness?" Harbinger dismissed the controller, who quickly took his seat.

The husky controller took his place on the stand, and Harbinger continued questioning about the tower's operations on that fateful day.

"The record shows that you used to work at O'Hare. When did you move to San Diego?" Harbinger asked.

"Six months ago, he replied."

"And you worked Approach at the Miramar Naval base?"

"Yes, Sir, Montgomery and Gillespie field too. They're all very close."

"So, you were reasonably familiar with most of the civil air traffic in the area?"

"Yes, and the military at the base."

"But not the jet routes at Lindbergh?" Harbinger was leading to something.

"I know the commercial air space, sir." The controller defended.

"But you hadn't worked in San Diego at Lindbergh?"

"No."

As the novice controller admitted his inexperience, Imani looked on, her face a mask of calm amidst the storm.

Harbinger continued. "How many days were you the sole controller of that tower?"

"As the assistant, I had done it for a month."

"Not as an assistant." He interrupted. "As the tower controller, calling the shots. How long?"

He was nervous. He looked at Lester Stone for support. Stone was sweating. Imani watched over the proceedings deadpan.

"That was my first time."

Harbinger slammed a book shut to make a point.

"If this inquiry has its way, this could be your last," Harbinger announced ominously, bringing his book down with a finality that echoed in the silent room.

After the hearing adjourned, Imani and Harbinger remained behind, their tension palpable.

"If the FAA's hands were clean, it wouldn't bother me so much. But they're not," Harbinger admitted, his voice laced with frustration.

"Those controllers did nothing wrong," Imani retorted, her gaze unyielding.

"I know that, but I need to establish beyond a reasonable doubt that there's not even a remote possibility for anyone to point the finger at the Administration," Harbinger argued, his eyes meeting Imani's.

"No one's pointing," Imani said, her voice calm yet firm. The room fell silent again, the echoes of the hearing still lingering in the air.

"Oh, they're out there. Believe me. We leave one stone unturned, one fact not checked. You deliver our findings and say the plane just fell right out of the sky. Gee whiz, isn't that amazing? They'll throw you to the lions, and you know why? Because the public wants to know what happened. They need someone to blame," Harbinger argued, his eyes alight with cynical wisdom born of years navigating the murky waters of law and public sentiment.

"That's not it. They just want to feel safe. Like you and me, they want the truth. They want to know that when their husbands or children get on a plane, and they go to the airport to pick them up, the worst problem they'll have is missing luggage," Imani countered, her voice carrying the resonance of earnest conviction.

"I'm telling you, Imani, we've got to deliver a bad guy," Harbinger insisted, drumming his fingers on the table.

"Who gets blamed when there's an earthquake? Who do we deliver then, huh? God?" Imani retorted, her gaze steady on Harbinger.

"An earthquake is not man-made. An airplane is," Harbinger replied, matching her steady gaze with his own.

"I just want to find out what went wrong," Imani stated, quiet but resolute.

"No, you want more. I can sense it. You blow this one, and your short-lived political career will be just that," Harbinger observed, leaning back in his chair, studying Imani with a critical eye.

"I'm not running for public office," Imani dismissed, her tone firm.

"Someone's got to be held accountable," Harbinger continued, his voice a steady rumble of insistence.

"And you don't care who?" Imani queried, her eyebrows arching in question.

"So long as it's not me," Harbinger replied with a chuckle, revealing a flash of white teeth in his otherwise stern demeanor.

"Who do you think is responsible?" Imani prodded, tilting her head as she studied Harbinger.

"That's your job, Chairman. We get you the facts," Harbinger replied, deflecting the question with a nonchalant shrug.

"I wouldn't be going too far, would I? I mean, legally speaking," Imani questioned, looking at Harbinger for reassurance.

"Hell no. That's what they want you to do," Harbinger affirmed, nodding his approval.

"You don't think I'm being too pushy? Overly zealous?" Imani asked, a hint of uncertainty in her voice.

"I'll let you know when you get too pushy. Do you want my advice?" Harbinger asked, raising his eyebrows in question.

"That's what we pay you for," Imani confirmed, her voice returning to its previous tone of resolve.

"Find the cause. The actual cause. And don't worry about stepping on some bastard's toes. Just go all the way. I'll let you know if it gets too hot," Harbinger concluded, leaning back in his chair, his gaze steady on Imani's determined face.

19

The night was enshrouded with stars as a cab pulled into the driveway of the iconic Del Coronado Hotel. Imani paid the driver inside the vehicle, exhaustion written in her eyes. Juggling a briefcase, a newspaper, and a stack of folders, she ascended the hotel's main steps and entered the warm glow of the lobby.

After collecting her messages from the front desk, she went to the dining room. Fraser had already seated himself there, enjoying what seemed like the best seat in the house. The room was subtly lit, comfortable, and not overly crowded. Imani approached his table. Her tiredness was apparent.

"Hungry?" Fraser asked, a warm look in his eyes.

"I'll just grab a sandwich," she replied, struggling to suppress a yawn.

"I just ordered dinner," he said, looking at her with a knowing grin.

"No, really, I'm fine."

"For two."

Imani cast a glance around the room, surprised. Fraser was alone.

"You're that hungry?" she quipped.

Fraser reached out, gently motioning her toward the chair opposite him. "Come on. It's your favorite."

"My favorite?" She allowed him to guide her into the seat, laying her belongings aside, her exhaustion momentarily forgotten.

Sometime later, the pair were wrapping up their meal. Imani wiped her mouth with a napkin, acknowledging with a satisfied sigh, "Okay, that was my favorite."

"I told you I remembered," Fraser replied, a smug satisfaction on his face.

"What was it?"

"The special," he responded.

As the night deepened, they shared stories from their past over a glass of wine. The atmosphere was light and convivial. Fraser mentioned an old memory. The server poured more wine. Both Imani and Fraser looked like they were enjoying this break from the stressful investigation. She, somewhat reluctantly.

"I remember when you used to skin your knees, and my brother would run you over with his wagon." Fraser reminisced.

Laughter erupted from Imani at the memory.

She shared the time at Christmas when Fraser received a battery-operated helicopter. "I remember when your father loved it so much; he broke it while playing with it, and you cried."

"I never cried," Fraser argued, playful indignation coloring his voice.

"Yes, you did."

"Never. You're confusing me with little Ricky Blair," Fraser retorted.

"I don't think so, Fraser," Imani responded, a nostalgic glint in her eyes. "You were wearing your cute little blue shorts and yellow suspenders, and you started crying like a baby when the rotor fell off."

Fraser, feeling the sting of defeat, chuckled and surrendered. "I knew I shouldn't have invited you over that year."

In the late evening, Imani and Fraser strolled past the hotel's closed shops, their laughter echoing through the quiet colonnade.

"Do you remember the time we went up to the lake?" Imani began, a wide grin spreading across her face. "Your mother wore that hat that looked like a robin's nest, and you'd put real eggs in it."

She was overcome with laughter at the memory, the sound bouncing off the walls. Fraser couldn't help but join her, his laughter mingling with hers.

"And when she crushed them all over her head," Imani continued, tears of mirth streaming down her cheeks, "your father thought it was her new perm."

She caught her breath, wiping the tears from her eyes. Fraser, still chuckling, nodded, acknowledging the absurdity of the memory.

"I always thought your parents were a little weird. Fun but weird," she confessed.

"Well, they sure liked you," Fraser replied, reminiscing about their shared past.

"The look on your face when you took me to the senior prom. You picked me up, my father asked what your intentions were, and you said you didn't have any. He was kidding, and you turned beet red."

"Yeah, your dad was quite a kidder. Had me going, I can tell you that. I thought I was destined for the priesthood that night," said Fraser.

"The innocence of youth. I miss it, don't you?" She asked.

"I have some pretty fond memories of those times."

"It wasn't always perfect."

A couple of guests glanced at the interracial couple. Music was playing in the background, and the server passed by.

"Excuse me, but what's that music? It sounds like a live band." Fraser asked.

The server turned to him. "It is. There's a wedding reception in the main ballroom."

Fraser and Imani exchanged a familiar look.

As they walked, the faint sound of music grew louder. Curious, they followed the sound, eventually leading them to a grand ballroom where a wedding reception was in full swing.

A formal dress code presided over the event. A rainbow of colors filled the grand ballroom. Black and white, brass, oak, ivory, and silk framed the unique colors the roses and corsages added to the night. The band was nestled on the stage, each musician hidden behind a gold and white-trimmed bandstand. Around them, couples swayed to the rhythm of the music, lost in the melodies. The big band played the most popular songs of all time.

"I wonder if we know anyone here?" Imani asked as they entered.

"Maybe we'll bump into someone from the past," Fraser replied. Despite their business attire, they fit seamlessly into the crowd of formally dressed guests.

"Shall we?" Fraser asked, extending his arm to Imani.

· · ·

The room was filled, and everyone was dancing, including Imani and Fraser. They found themselves swept up in the joyous atmosphere, their bodies moving in time to the music. They laughed and twirled, their movements easy and familiar.

The dance ended, and they stood silently, each lost in thought. The music started again, and they began to dance, bodies moving in harmony with the rhythm. Fraser broke the silence, his voice filled with regret. "I could kick myself for letting you go."

His confession took Imani by surprise. "Really?" she asked.

"Yeah," Fraser confessed, a mixture of regret and longing on his face. "I didn't realize it until your wedding. Standing there, shaking hands with your new husband. I wished it was me."

A silence fell between them, punctuated only by the surrounding music. He admitted to his past mistakes, loneliness, and regret for not committing to her. His words hung in the air, the echoes of a past that could have been.

He glanced away.

"Then I got in my Corvette and drove home. Alone. All two hundred and fifty miles that night. I had a lot of time to think. I knew I wouldn't see you again and kicked myself for not having the guts."

"To do what?" she asked.

"To commit. To ask you to marry me. I always thought there'd be someone else, maybe someone better." He whispered reluctantly.

"Someone different. More like you?"

"I was wrong. It was the loneliest night of my life."

The music stopped. The lights dimmed. They stared at each other for an extended moment. And softly, the emcee announced. "Ladies and gentlemen, this will be the last dance of the night."

Slowly, softly, the band began. The couples paired off and started dancing a last waltz. Imani and Fraser joined in.

Fraser looked lovingly at Imani. "I have one last question. Been bugging me for twenty years. What did I do wrong?" He asked.

"So many things." She sighed.

"Really?"

"But one stood out. You disappointed me. You underestimated yourself, and you underestimated me."

He didn't take this well, almost not wanting to believe it because he felt he tried so hard. But he recovered and barely showed his sadness.

"How?"

"You hurt me. With other girls."

"You didn't give me enough time, that's all. I just needed a little more time." Fraser pleaded.

"I never thought you would clean up your act. You were too careless with us."

"I thought you liked that fun, reckless quality."

"Fraser, I was young too. I had stardust in my eyes. I didn't need to be hurt like that by the things you did. It just made me think you didn't care. You didn't really understand."

"But I did care."

"You didn't care enough."

"I didn't know how to show it."

"I believed you would never change," she admitted.

"Imani, I loved you. I'd be a different person if I were with you now."

"I couldn't wait for you to change." She confessed.

Fraser paused, looked her in the eye, and said, "I still love you."

It was a conversation filled with heartache and lost opportunities. They held each other tightly, the world swirling around them. Their shared past and present collided in that one extended moment. The music swirled around them, a bittersweet symphony to their lost love.

20

The night had settled around the hotel, its white verandas and red tile roof imbuing it with a storybook charm. Imani and Fraser strolled arm in arm, the distant pounding of the surf resonating in the stillness of the night.

"I used to always tell you what to do," Fraser began, a hint of irony creeping into his voice. "What to wear, how to act, what to say. Now you're telling me. Just goes to show you I didn't know what the hell I was talking about."

Imani turned to look at him, her eyes catching the soft glow of the moonlight. A moment of tension hung between them, mirrored by the turbulent sea and the whispering wind. Then, surrendering to the pull of the moment, they kissed.

"You know," Fraser murmured, pulling away slightly. "I never meant to hurt you."

"I know," she responded softly, the weight of their shared past evident in her tone.

They continued their walk along the sandy beach. The warm lights of the hotel glowed in the distance, casting a soft golden hue on the shoreline. Noticing Imani's shivering form, Fraser quickly shrugged off his jacket and draped it around her shoulders.

"Are you cold?" he asked, though her trembling body answered him already.

"No," she lied, but she didn't protest when he wrapped his coat around her.

"Is there any chance for us?" Fraser asked, his tone hopeful yet unsure.

"It's complicated," Imani answered, her voice tinged with sadness.

Fraser shook his head slightly, his expression serious. "It doesn't have to be."

"But it is," she insisted. "I'm happy. I'm married. I have a family. I don't have any regrets."

"But what about passion?" he queried, desperation beginning to creep into his voice.

"I have a husband and children I love," she reminded him, her voice soft. "It'd be so hard on them. On everyone."

Fraser pressed on, relentless. "What if it was a mistake? All you're doing is realizing you made a mistake."

Her reply was quiet and filled with a touch of admiration. "That's one thing I always admired about you. You fall down, get up, brush yourself off, and start all over again. I get a run in my stocking. It's the end of the world. That's the difference between you and me."

Fraser tried a different angle. "So what do you say? Why can't you be more like me, and I'll be more like you?"

She shook her head. "It doesn't work like that."

"I'm asking you to give me one last shot, Imani," Fraser pleaded. "I'm asking you just to consider it. I swear I won't let you down."

Imani's response was a soft sigh. "I'm flattered. I wish we

could go back in time, but we can't. Look, it's late, and I'm freezing, and we're both a little drunk."

Hope sparked in Fraser's eyes. "Then you'll come to Mexico with me?" His question hung between them, lingering like the sea salt mist.

The morning sun lent a gleaming radiance to the city's landmark hotel. Red-peaked roofs and white cabanas stood starkly beautiful against the backdrop of the azure Pacific Ocean.

Inside one of the hotel rooms, the shrill sound of a phone pierced the quiet. Imani reached out from the depths of sleep, perhaps a hangover still clinging to her, to answer it. Still half-dreaming, she murmured, "Hello? Oh, hi hon. No, I'm fine. No, you didn't wake me. Just exhausted, I guess. Long week, yeah. Very long. Can I call you back in a few minutes? Okay."

She hung up, her lips brushing a soft kiss against the phone before it rang again. With a sigh, she picked it up once more. "Yes. What time is it? You are? Oh. Okay. Do I need to bring golf clubs cause I don't have any? Okay. Bye."

The moment the call ended, sleep claimed her again until a harsh alarm clock jerked her back into consciousness. She hurriedly gathered her belongings and rushed out of the hotel lobby, a couple of small bags swinging from her hand.

Her haste cost her a broken heel as she descended the hotel's main entrance stairs. She quickly caught herself on a railing, took off her shoes, and got into a waiting cab that hurried to her destination.

She arrived at the private jet terminal, paid the driver, and rushed inside. Swiftly moving through security, she left her belongings on a conveyor belt and passed through the gate without incident. Once in the departure lounge, she peered out of a large window, spotting Fraser on the apron, shaking hands with a U.S. Customs agent while a pit crew prepared the Lear 35 jet for takeoff.

Imani darted towards the exit, making her way barefoot onto the apron. Fraser waved to her from the jet's flight deck. She hurried past the customs agent and climbed a few steps, stopping right before getting on the plane.

What am I doing? Just going to play an innocent game of golf, she reassured herself. Satisfied with her reasoning, she tossed her scarf over her shoulder and boarded the idling Lear jet.

Once inside, she dropped her bags onto a seat and moved towards the flight deck, where Fraser was alone at the controls. The jet was already beginning to roll.

"Hi. You better buckle up. We'll be in the wild blue yonder any second," Fraser greeted her.

"Where's the pilot?" Imani asked, glancing around the cockpit.

"I gave him the day off," Fraser replied nonchalantly.

"To test your flying ability?" she questioned, looking at him dubiously.

"Sort of. You know these babies cruise at 500 knots. Pretty fast, huh?" Fraser boasted, drawing her attention to the panel's array of switches and dials.

"I'm surprised you don't have a CD player," Imani said, touching some panel switches.

"What do you want to hear?" Fraser asked, flipping a switch. A *Bruce Springsteen* rock beat suddenly drowned out the radio chatter, adding energy to the jet's acceleration.

"You can't hear the tower," Imani pointed out.

"But I can hear you," Fraser reassured her.

"Fraser, where are your friends?" Imani asked, confusion wrinkling her brow.

"What friends?" Fraser asked.

"The ones we're supposed to be going to play golf with? In Mexico, remember?" Imani reminded him.

"Oh yeah, those friends. Well, they called at the last minute and decided they couldn't make it," Fraser admitted, flashing her a wide grin.

"So, who else is going?" she pressed, a note of concern creeping into her voice.

"Just you and me, babes," Fraser replied, his grin sheepish.

"You and me, babes? Babes?" Imani echoed, a note of discomfort evident in her voice.

As the plane continued to taxi, Imani spotted a woman's silk crotchless camisole stuffed under Fraser's seat. Retrieving it, she held it up for him to see. "Anyone we know?" she asked, a challenge in her eyes.

"Cleaning crew must have left it," Fraser replied, clearly caught off guard.

"Stop the plane. I want off," Imani demanded, but Fraser ignored her plea, insisting they were too close to takeoff to stop now.

"Come on, we're almost at the threshold. I can't stop now," he said.

"Stop the plane. I want to get off."

"Imani, don't be ridiculous. We're thirty seconds from takeoff."

In defiance, Imani rose from her seat and slammed her hand against a panel of switches. "I said, stop the plane. I want off," she demanded again. She stuffed the camisole over his head. The plane started to swerve. She pulled back hard on the yoke, slamming it into his chest.

"You can't get off," Fraser tried to argue, but Imani was not to be deterred.

With a fire in her eyes, she shoved Fraser, dislodging him from the controls. "Stop the plane. I want off now," she demanded, her voice cold and unwavering, leaving no room for Fraser to argue.

The airplane skidded to a halt, a testament to the intense scene that had just occurred. Imani, her luggage in tow, trudged along the taxiway. She glanced back just in time to see the Learjet align itself with the centerline, gaining speed on its takeoff roll until it was a speck in the sky.

21

Days later, the atmosphere inside the formal hearing room buzzed with tension and anticipation. Imani was talking quietly with some victims' families when Fraser, wearing sunglasses, entered with a group of corporate attorneys. A quick exchange of icy stares spoke volumes of their animosity.

Harbinger rose from his seat. Approaching a giant whiteboard, he drew a line at the bottom of the board. He placed a tower line at one end, then put first one, then a second line in the air. The diagrams marked critical points of the doomed flight's trajectory. His findings painted a grim picture; Paragon 860's engine failure and the proximity of other planes had all contributed to the catastrophic event.

He began. "When Paragon 860 flew into San Diego airspace, they were here. They proceeded inbound for fifteen more miles, and it was at this point that the airplane first experienced trouble. In less than a minute, it lost all power and broke down because of engine failure and metal fatigue."

Fraser folded his arms, barely listening.

"A second plane was also in the immediate area, over here.

Just inside the edge of the TCA." Harbinger continued as he drew an arc. "It was presumed that we had the makings of a mid-air collision. However, records show that the Paragon flight was at 7,500 feet, and this plane, a Piper Cherokee, was at 8,000. A difference of five hundred feet."

Fraser whispered to a crony. "Amazing. He can subtract."

There was a murmur in the crowd.

"What further mystified investigators was a third airplane recovered from the ocean floor directly below the impact zone. We discovered this was a stolen aircraft off the radar flying at a hundred feet over the ocean. It was outside the control zone. He was, therefore, in uncontrolled airspace." Harbinger stated.

Fraser was bored, ready to fall asleep.

"When we get to the part where the Pilgrims land at Plymouth Rock, let me know." He smiled. This elicited a laugh.

Imani scolded him. "Mr. Gillingham, you can leave any time you want."

"No, Chairman, I think this part will be very interesting." He yawned. Imani nodded for Harbinger to continue.

Harbinger took a breath. "Now, aside from the general underwater damage on the plane, the only area of impact was on the starboard aileron, which, for the public record, was the back of the right wing. Two things perplexed examiners. One, planes don't fly backward. Two, the damage on the aileron was man-made and happened after the crash."

The crowd murmured over this one. Fraser started paying attention. Imani noticed this.

"Registration records revealed that the plane was owned by a small FBO in Texas called Signet Aviation. Business licenses and state records showed that Signet Aviation was owned by three partners, one of whom was Mr. Gillingham, president of Paragon Airlines."

There was an uproar.

As the implications of this revelation resonated around the

room, Fraser was caught off-guard, hurriedly conferring with his attorneys. An audible murmur spread amongst the crowd, punctuated by the rhythmic tap of Imani's gavel. Initially filled with uncertainty and sorrow, the hearing had taken a dramatic turn, and all eyes were fixed on Fraser.

22

A s the hours wore on, an attendant wheeled Captain Finicky into the room in a wheelchair. Fraser leaned over to whisper to his attorney, eyebrows furrowed in surprise.

"What the hell is he doing here?"

"If they can get the whole thing over in one shot, it'll save them time later on," the attorney replied, trying to keep his voice even.

Imani's gavel echoed in the room, pulling attention back to her. "This hearing is back in session."

Harbinger took over again, his tone serious as he addressed Captain Finicky. "Captain Finicky, how long have you flown for Paragon?"

"Ever since I left the service. Thirty-five years," Finicky responded, his voice steady despite his frail state.

"And would you consider yourself a loyal employee?" Harbinger continued, his gaze steady on the elderly pilot.

"More than most," was the calm reply.

"With a strong sense of safety, no doubt?"

"Yes."

Harbinger referenced the regulations on pilot responsibility for aircraft safety and sought confirmation from Finicky.

"Under FAR section 43.71, does it not state that the pilot in command of a commercial aircraft must ensure that his aircraft is safe for public transport, otherwise he is in violation of that section and would risk having his license revoked?" Harbinger asked.

"Yes, it does say that."

"With a strong sense of safety, no doubt?"

"Yes."

"So were you then not in violation of Part 43 by flying an aircraft that you knew beforehand was not only unsafe but was many hours, one hundred and fifty in fact, past its time before engine overhaul?" Harbinger challenged.

"No, it was only fifteen," Finicky replied.

"Captain, we have authenticated statements on all activity on that plane, and it was one hundred fifty hours past due—an amount that would deem that aircraft unsafe to fly."

Though shaken by the line of questioning, the captain admitted to his awareness of these regulations. But as Harbinger accused him of knowingly flying an unsafe plane, an aircraft overdue for engine overhaul by a staggering one hundred and fifty hours, Finicky vehemently denied it.

"No, that's not right," he insisted, looking at Fraser for support. "It was only fifteen." However, Harbinger presented the documented evidence, claiming the plane was significantly overdue for maintenance, which stunned the captain.

"And despite that and knowing the risk beforehand, you proceeded to fly that plane, resulting in the deaths of over one hundred and eighty-one passengers. Is that not true?"

"No."

Harbinger allowed the room to settle and Finicky to compose himself.

Harbinger then asked the crucial question, "Captain

Finicky, you were an experienced pilot with a commendable record. For the sake of this inquiry, can you tell us why you flew that plane to San Diego?"

"I didn't want to. I told the dispatcher that, Sam Icarus," Finicky answered, his voice shaky.

"And what did he say?" Harbinger probed further.

"He got Mr. Gillingham on the line," the captain revealed.

Harbinger seized upon this information. "Isn't that a little unusual? Calling the airline's president to settle a matter that could generally be handled right there or escalated through the proper channels like ALPA, the Pilots' Union, for instance?"

"Mr. Gillingham didn't want me to go to the union. He told me once before that if there was ever a serious problem, he wanted to be personally notified," Finicky revealed, adding another unexpected twist to the tale.

"So, Mr. Gillingham knew the plane was past due?" Harbinger pressed.

"Yes, sir," Finicky confirmed as all eyes turned to Fraser.

"And what did Mr. Gillingham say?" Harbinger asked, a victorious glint in his eyes.

Imani listened intently, sizing Fraser up.

Finicky's voice wavered as he echoed Fraser's words, "He said that planes were a lot like cars, and not everybody changed their oil every six thousand miles."

"An engine overhaul on a commercial jetliner is a whole different ballgame from an oil change on your family sedan, Captain," Harbinger countered, his voice ringing with certainty.

"Yes, but Mr. Gillingham was very convincing. He said when I got to San Diego, he'd take my wife and me to dinner." A nervous laugh erupted from the audience, momentarily splitting the room's tension.

Harbinger glanced at Imani for guidance and received a

nod in return. Fraser, however, wasn't as lucky. Despite his desperate appeal for mercy, Imani ignored him entirely.

"You live in San Diego, don't you, Captain?" Harbinger resumed his interrogation.

"Yes."

"And this was the last flight of your career. In fact, you were retiring, weren't you?"

"Yes."

"And you wanted to get home to your family, didn't you?"

"Yes."

"So badly, in fact, that you were willing to risk your life and the lives of your passengers and crew, weren't you?"

"No!" Finicky wailed.

With a nod, Harbinger ended his questioning. "No further questions."

Imani rose from her seat, her voice cutting through the silence. "This hearing will adjourn for one hour. We will reconvene at two o'clock."

As the room slowly emptied, Fraser turned to his counsel. "Poor bastard's crucifying himself," he muttered, his gaze still fixed on Captain Finicky's departing figure.

23

The city park was dappled with sunlight, and a deli across the street bustled with the lunchtime crowd. Fraser found Imani on a park bench, a solemn figure amidst the casual enjoyment of the day.

"Can I buy you lunch?" he asked, sitting beside her.

"I don't have much of an appetite, thanks," she responded, her gaze fixed on the distant movement of pedestrians.

"My offer still holds," he pressed, determined to break through her calm exterior.

"It'd be a serious conflict of interest," she countered.

"I mean, after all this," he clarified, leaning back on the bench, "Imani, all I need is a good woman like you to straighten me out."

"Maybe you think you're right," she agreed, her tone noncommittal.

"Sure I am. I'm not some devil. I'm just a guy like any guy with drives and desires. I've made my share of mistakes," he confessed, meeting her gaze.

"We all have, Fraser. I don't want to make any more either, and I don't want to hurt you personally," she admitted.

"Don't worry. Whatever you decide, I can handle it," he reassured her.

"Can you?" she asked, studying him intently.

"Look, I know things might be tough for a few quarters, but we'll get past it. We'll just raise the fares and pass the fine along to the public. Build it into the cost," he explained confidently.

"What makes you think the government will fine you? The hearing hasn't reached its conclusion yet," she reminded him, a hint of challenge in her tone.

"They've got to. That's what the government is supposed to do. Send us a hefty bill for being bad boys," he said with a touch of gallows humor. His following words seemed to spill out in a gush, a detailed, cynical vision of how the coming crisis could be weathered. "The insurance company pays off the claimants. We drag the settlements through the courts for years. Of course, we appeal it. Play tennis for a while, then cut our ad campaign for six months, chop some heads, unload some lowbrow suppliers, and see if we can lay the rest off on the manufacturer and the frequent flyers. It's all a game."

"And life goes on?" she asked, sounding almost despairing.

"That's right. Life goes on," he confirmed with a grim sort of cheerfulness.

"What about remedying the problem?" Imani asked.

"We're deregulated now. You just tell me what you want us to do. We'll do it."

"Fraser, the '78 Act did not diminish the FAA's power over air safety."

"Yeah. Thanks to Carter."

"So, don't you know what to do?"

"I'm not sure what you mean." He looked puzzled.

"What if I just let you off the hook?"

Fraser paused. "Imani, that would be too kind. I don't want any special favors. Just treat me the same as everybody else," he stated.

"What if it hurts the airline?"

"The only thing that could hurt me is losing you, and that's already happened," Fraser admitted.

"Well, what if it hurts me?" She asked.

"That's what you're faced with?"

"Yes," she said.

"It's terrible, isn't it?" He glanced at people nearby.

She nodded. "Very."

"What about us?" Fraser asked.

"Unlikely," she said when Fraser asked.

The conversation continued, a dance of rhetoric and rebuttal, of old hurts and new realities. But in the end, it was Imani who delivered the final blow.

She got up from the bench and walked away, her last words hanging in the air. "It's too late for that now."

"Imani? Imani?" Fraser called after her, but she kept walking, leaving him alone on the park bench.

"If I'd married her twenty-five years ago, this never would have happened," he muttered to himself, a lone figure watching the woman he lost walk away.

24

The formal hearing room buzzed back to life as everyone returned to their seats. Fraser Gillingham, confident and bold, approached Imani at the bench. "Could we just move right along with this? I've got a tennis match at three," he asked, a note of impatience in his voice.

"Don't worry. It won't take long," Chairman Safe assured him, her tone equally relaxed and professional.

"Appreciate it," Fraser responded, offering a half-hearted grin before retreating to his seat. His attorneys were already ushering two young women down the aisle—his new girl-friends, clad in tennis outfits. One was Asian, the other an exotic Brazilian. They settled next to him, drawing curious glances and hushed whispers from the room. Fraser, unbothered by the attention, gave them each a quick kiss. The room finally settled, ready to resume.

"Would Randolph Fix please come forward?" Harbinger requested.

A mechanic, whose suit seemed to struggle against his robust form, lumbered into the room, clutching a greasy-looking journal.

"Mr. Fix, could you tell us what happened before flight 860 left San Francisco on the night of January the nineteenth?" Harbinger asked, looking down at his notes.

"I guess you can tell by looking at me that I'm an airplane mechanic, and I'm proud to be one, too," Fix started, his voice rough but confident.

"Randy, why don't you tell us about your mother's home-made apple pie?" Fraser interjected, eliciting a few chuckles from the room.

Fix looked genuinely surprised but quickly recovered. "Oh, my mother makes great apple pie, doesn't she, Mr. Gillingham?"

"She sure does," Fraser agreed, leaning back in his chair, looking smug.

"Mr. Gillingham? Please," Imani reprimanded, bringing the room's focus back to the matter at hand.

"Sorry, ma'am. You really ought to try it sometime. The best," Fraser continued, clearly enjoying himself.

Harbinger looked a bit flustered but regained his composure quickly. "Mr. Fix, tell us what you already said in your sworn statement," he prompted.

Fraser leaned over to whisper to one of his attorneys, "Statements?" The attorney merely shrugged, leaving Fraser looking perplexed. Meanwhile, Fix was consulting his journal, preparing to recount the events of the night in question.

"Well, we were pretty busy that day when I came to work. I think when that flight came in, we already had ten other planes on the ramp," Fix began.

"Is that more than usual?" Harbinger questioned, sounding genuinely interested.

"Oh yeah, most we'd see at one time would be five or six, and they'd be staggered," Fix explained. He seemed to grow more comfortable with every passing moment.

"Why were there so many that day?" Harbinger asked.

"Big snowstorm in the Rockies. I guess they kept hoping that the weather would clear. All that happened was they kept holding all those flights on the wheel."

"On the wheel?"

"Yeah, like the wheel of a bicycle. The spokes and the wheel. We were on the wheel," Fix informed him.

"Did that put a strain on your resources?"

Fraser stood up abruptly, interrupting the flow of the testimony. "I object to this line of questioning. He's leading the witness," he argued.

"This isn't a courtroom, Mr. Gillingham," Imani reminded him, a note of exasperation in her voice.

"Just so long as we all know that, Chairman Safe," Fraser shot back, reclaiming his seat and bracing himself for whatever would come next.

Harbinger persisted, determined to get straightforward answers. "I'll rephrase the question for the record. Mr. Fix, how would you describe the allocation of resources at the airport that day?"

Fraser was on his feet again. "I object. He can't possibly know what allocation of resources means."

"Mr. Gillingham, you don't have the floor," Imani interrupted, her patience wearing thin.

"Screw the floor. Ask the man a question he understands," Fraser retorted, gesturing dramatically toward Fix.

But Fix was no wallflower. "Mr. Gillingham, I may be only a flying grease monkey in your eyes, but I know how to read and write, and I think I can answer that question on my own, sir." Fraser had to accept this and sank back into his chair.

Harbinger composed himself and tried once more. "For the third time, Mr. Fix. How would you describe resource allocation in your area in San Francisco that day?"

"Strained," Fix replied succinctly.

· · ·

As the day wore on, a pit crew mechanic took the stand. The mechanic's testimony was particularly telling. Harbinger inquired, "When you told the flight engineer that one tire had a slow leak, what did he say?"

"He said to fix it," the mechanic answered.

"And did you?" Harbinger pressed.

"No time."

"How long did he give you to repair the leaking tire?"

"Five minutes."

"And how long would that task typically take?"

"We'd have to unload the plane first."

"How long?" Harbinger persisted.

"An hour," the mechanic admitted.

The Director of Operations found himself on the stand as the sun set. Harbinger, tireless and unrelenting, began his line of questioning. "You were on duty the day Captain Finicky requested a new plane, is that right?"

"Yes."

"And he requested it from you?"

"Through the dispatcher."

"Why didn't you give him another aircraft?"

"We didn't have any we could release at the time."

"But Mr. Fix just told us you had several extra planes, at least four others in San Francisco, that you could have used," Harbinger pointed out, his voice echoing through the silent room.

The man leading operations appeared somewhat defensive as he explained, "The way things look on the ground and the way they actually are are often two different things. A mechanic in the field is not going to know about other demands on the fleet."

"So, while those four extra planes sat for another full day

and the storm continued, did you have other demands for those same planes?" Harbinger probed further.

"No." His monosyllabic response echoed through the room, causing Fraser to shift uncomfortably in his chair.

"Let me ask you something else. In his written statement, Mr. Fix referred to the Spoke and Wheel. Could you explain that to us?" Harbinger continued, unperturbed. The man seemed an unwilling witness, casting an uneasy glance toward Fraser.

"We move the aircraft around a central hub," he explained, voice strained.

"And that central hub is where?"

"Denver."

"And that's where you work?"

"Yes. Most of the planes fly through the hub all the time. We have a couple of flights a day from Denver to Santa Barbara and back or Denver and Houston. From the center to the wheel and back."

"Along the spokes?"

"Yes, exactly. That way, we can keep a good eye on the aircraft and ensure it gets its 'C' check. It's an annual checkup when it hits a specific number of flight hours, FH, for short."

"And every plane gets this?" Harbinger pursued, leaning slightly forward.

"Yes. Takes about a week. It's a comprehensive series of tests, including the 'Eddy Current' test, which will turn up cracks in the thrust reversers. All our planes pass with flying colors."

"You have an extensive fleet, though, don't you?"

"Yes, we do. Six hundred and thirty-nine aircraft."

"You must be proud of that. Your public record shows that you are the number one air carrier and that your traffic rose by twenty-three percent from the prior year while your load factor grew to a healthy eighty-nine percent, well above the industry norm."

"Mr. Gillingham is mostly responsible for that increase," he remarked, sending a deferential nod Fraser's way.

"I'm sure he is. Tell me something. With the planes in the air most of the time and some of them always on the wheel, is there a chance that when it came time for its 'C' check, one might slip through the crack?"

"No, sir, we're computerized." His declaration relieved almost everyone in the room, save for Harbinger and Imani. They exchanged a glance, and she silently indicated for him to proceed.

"I have the flight log for Flight 860 for the last three months before the accident. Let me read it to you." Harbinger recited the extensive list, each destination adding to the undeniable discrepancy in the company's records. "Seattle to San Francisco. San Francisco to L.A., L.A. to Phoenix. Phoenix to San Diego. San Diego to Phoenix. And on and on. In fact, nowhere is there any record of this plane going into Denver. Looking further back, it's been seven months since flight 860 even entered the hub for repairs."

Imani and Fraser exchanged a chillingly silent exchange.

Harbinger continued, challenging the math behind their operations. "And this is not an isolated case. My calculations show that with a fleet your size, if it takes a week for a 'C' check, you would always have at least 12 aircraft in Denver year-round that are out of service. Now, if we count the short-term delays due to mechanical failure, it would be impossible with a reduced working fleet of 568 aircraft to maintain an 89% utilization factor. The numbers don't add up."

Caught off guard, the director scrambled for an explanation. "Sometimes on short hauls and particularly with an older plane, we want to keep them in a good weather area," he attempted to reason. Still, the skeptical faces around the room suggested that this response fell far short of a satisfying explanation.

"Then how would it ever get serviced?" Harbinger challenged, his voice measured yet persistent.

"In the wheel cities," the Director of Operations replied, a touch of defensiveness tinting his tone.

"With the strained resources that Mr. Fix just told us about?"

"You do whatever it takes."

"Whatever it takes. What does that mean?"

"I'm afraid I don't understand."

"Has this plane been serviced? If so, when?" Harbinger continued, relentless in his pursuit. The Director of Operations shuffled through a set of documents, his fingers landing on a particular sheet.

"It says right here. We had that flight in Denver Center on October 15th and August 8th before that."

"And work was done on the aircraft?"

"Yes, sir."

"By your staff?"

"The repair station, sir."

"If that's the case, can you explain why there are no work orders, materials, or parts requisitions and no record, in fact, of any payment being made from Denver for that plane?"

"No, I can't explain that, sir. Must be an accounting problem."

"An accounting problem?"

"Yes, sir."

"You're sure. Accounting?"

"That's right, sir."

A break was called in the hearing. The hallway buzzed with chatter. Fraser Gillingham, accompanied by his lieutenants, board, and attorneys, carried an air of confidence bordering on arrogance, seemingly convinced that the hearing would result in little consequence.

25

Later, in the formal hearing room, the tension thickened as Harbinger called Fraser to the stand. Imani maintained her control over the proceedings, watching the interaction with a stern expression.

"Mr. Gillingham," Harbinger began, addressing Fraser with a professional tone, "do you believe that the responsibilities of a company president are to discharge his duties for the private good?"

Fraser's eyebrows arched upwards. "I'm not under oath, am I?"

Harbinger shook his head. "No, sir."

"Private good?" Fraser parroted, a hint of disdain in his voice.

"Yes."

"Absolutely," Fraser declared. "It's the stockholders' assets we're managing. The little widows and orphans."

"So," Harbinger continued, "then you also believe that management should be held accountable for their actions and rewarded for their performance?"

"Capitalistic meritocracy," Fraser retorted. "That's the name of the game. They aren't thinking of firing me, are they?" His remark elicited a smattering of laughter from the crowd.

"Seeing as you own a large share of the company and sit on the Board of Directors, I hardly think so," Harbinger replied, a hint of dry humor in his voice.

"You had me worried there for a second. Rent is due," Fraser quipped before he was dismissed from the stand. As he moved to return to his seat, Harbinger had another question.

"Mr. Gillingham, one final question," he called out.

Fraser paused. "You want me to come up there again?"

"That's not necessary," Harbinger replied. "Some say that you rule your company with an iron fist. Would you agree with that statement?"

Fraser glanced at his hand and held it up. "Does this look like iron to you?"

"Let me rephrase that," Harbinger persisted. "Do you know everything that's going on in your company?"

Fraser shot a glance towards his counsel, beckoning him over. They exchanged whispered comments. The counsel, sensing the danger of the situation, urged Fraser to be cautious.

"Careful what you say. This guy could slaughter you." He was advised.

"He's just a second-rate government brown suit that studied law at a third-rate college. I don't mind playing a little hard-ball," Fraser replied.

"He's looking for blood."

"Don't worry. I got an inside track with the NTSB. We go way back." He smiled at Imani, but the smile was not returned.

"Well, be careful. If you want, we can get you out of this. Just say the word." His attorney assured him.

However, with a final wink to his counsel, Fraser turned back to Harbinger and asked, "What was the question?"

"Are you aware of everything going on with your company?"

Harbinger repeated, maintaining his composure despite Fraser's antics.

"Well, outside of the flight attendants screwing the baggage handlers, I'd have to say 'yes,'" Fraser retorted smugly. "Although we do get monthly reports on personnel activity, and some of it's pretty juicy."

Imani commandeered the proceedings, "We will take a short break."

When the hearing reconvened, NTSB Chairman Imani Safe took control. "Would the following please stand? Mr. Rice, Mr. Hunter, Mr. Genesee, Mr. Clark, and Mr. Gillingham." As they rose to their feet, the tension in the room escalated.

"Gentlemen, a flagrant and utter disregard for the public safety leaves this hearing no alternative but to recommend the government fine the airline in an amount commensurate with sustained damages under Federal Aviation Administration and NTSB guidelines," she began, her voice calm and firm. Fraser couldn't help but smirk at his colleagues, clearly underestimating the gravity of the situation.

"It would be unfair to all concerned if the airline were asked to cease operations until the deficiencies are cured," Imani continued, feeding Fraser's misplaced sense of security. But her following words shattered his facade of confidence.

"Instead of that action, this committee will make a referral to the Securities and Exchange Commission and the Justice Department that charges of fraud, criminal negligence, and involuntary manslaughter are personally brought against the five men I have just named."

Chaos ensued, the room bursting into a flurry of voices. The accused men were stunned. Fraser yelled over the crowd, "You'll never get away with this."

"The full record of this hearing may be requested through the Department of Transportation in Washington."

Fraser pushed his way to the front of the room. Bailiffs restrained him.

"You're blowing smoke, lady. You haven't got a leg to stand on."

Over the din of the crowd, Imani declared, "This hearing is now adjourned." She stepped down and cast a last glance at Fraser, the man she used to love, her expression a mix of sorrow and resolve. As she walked away, Fraser shouted, "We'll file an appeal!" Fraser appeared completely shocked, never believing she could do this. "I tell you. We'll get an appeal," he shouted.

26

———

The next day, at the airport ticket counter, Lester escorted Imani as she booked a flight for Washington D.C. Reagan International. The ticket agent punched the keys at the terminal.

"Thanks for driving me, Lester."

"Pleasure's all mine," he replied.

The ticket agent interrupted. "The next flight leaves in an hour."

Imani seemed disappointed. "Nothing sooner?"

Lester glanced at the next counter. "Looks like Paragon has one leaving in ten minutes."

They looked at the counter. The Paragon brand colors identified the airline. There was no one in line. Three ticket agents twiddled their thumbs.

"No, I don't mind waiting," Imani said. "We can only afford one broken leg in the family."

Imani smiled. Lester shook her hand goodbye, and the

ticket agent gave Imani her ticket as she got ready to board the plane.

On October 19, 1987, Black Monday shocked the world with a stock market crash that caused Paragon Airlines to lose half its market cap in a single day. The airline filed for bankruptcy, never to recover.

Fraser Gillingham died in a plane crash two days later.

A control tower radar screen faded to black, leaving behind a somber silence.

REVIEW

If you liked this book, please fee free to leave an honest review. Thanks so much.

http://www.amazon.com/review/create-review?&asin= B0CC9DQ34F

ALSO BY A.C. JETT

AWARDS - SCREENPLAY

Crash Site

- Award Winner, 52 Weeks Film Festival, 2020
  - Finalist, Inroads Screenwriting Fellowship, 2020
  - Finalist, Las Vegas International Film & Screenwriting Festival, 2020
  - Finalist, Rocky Mountain International Film Festival, 2020
  - Top 20%, Academy Nicholl Fellowship, 2021
  - Top 20%, Academy Nicholl Fellowship, 2017
  - Semifinalist (Pilot), Los Angeles International Screenplay Awards, 2021
  - Semifinalist, Austin Screenplay Awards, 2020
  - Semifinalist, Your Script Produced! Studios: Season 2, 2021
  - Semifinalist, Austin Revolution Film Festival, 2020
  - Semifinalist, Loudoun Arts Film Festival, 2020
  - Semifinalist, Scriptation Showcase Script Competition, 2020
  - Semifinalist, TRMS Park City, 2020
  - Quarterfinalist, ScreenCraft Family Screenplay Competition, 2021
  - Quarterfinalist, Stage 32 Feature Drama Screenwriting Contest, 2020
  - Quarterfinalist, Santa Barbara International Screenplay Awards, 2021
  - Quarterfinalist, Los Angeles International Screenplay Awards, 2020
  - Quarterfinalist, Creative World Awards (Drama), 2020
  - Official Selection, Austin Revolution Film Festival, 2020

- Official Selection, Scriptation Showcase Script Competition, 2020
- Official Selection, Finish Line Script Competition, 2019
- Official Selection, Loudoun Arts Film Festival, 2020
- Official Selection, Marina del Rey Film Festival, 2020
- Official Selection, Las Vegas International Film & Screenwriting Festival, 2020
- Official Selection, European Independent Film Awards, 2021

FINAL APPEAL

Night cloaked San Quentin Prison, the notorious death row housing the worst of humanity. Two burly prison guards, muscles taut beneath their uniforms, escorted Santiago Vincent Branch, a serial killer of four decades, down the bleak, dim-lit corridor. The hardness etched on Branch's face was reflected in his lifeless, dark eyes. Mud clung stubbornly to his shoes, and his fingernails were filled with grime.

The macabre procession halted within the grim confines of the California Gas Chamber. A guard, identifiable by the knife scar marring his chin, broke the seal on the hatch, revealing a depressingly drab room bathed in an eerie green hue. Its steel shell housed two foreboding metal chairs at its heart.

They secured Branch, strapping him down with worn leather bindings around his wrists and ankles. The fastenings bit into his flesh, as tight as they could make them. A heart monitor was affixed to his chest, the rhythmic thudding echoing ominously in the quiet chamber. "Have a nice life," one of the guards sneered before the hatch was again sealed. A wall clock stared back at them, its hands teetering on the edge of 11:59 PM.

Inside his steel enclosure, Branch surveyed his surroundings. Beneath his seat, a pound of lethal sodium-cyanide pellets sat in a tank. Opaque windows loomed behind him, offering him no glimpse of what lay beyond. He twisted uncomfortably in his restraints and glared contemptuously at the unseen watchers.

A voice crackled to life over the intercom, "Any last words?" the unseen man asked.

Branch's gaze was predatory as he scanned the smoked glass. His retort was as venomous as it was terse, "FUCK YOU, Warden! And print that on the front page with all the letters, F-U-C-K."

Behind the obscured windows, the prison warden, Harry Slam, a hardened man in his fifties, exchanged a glance with Arlen Murkey, the Attorney General. At sixty, Murkey bore the air of a professor, albeit one with a noticeable hard edge.

"Guy's a genius. He can spell," Slam commented dryly.

"Save it, Harry," Murkey rebuffed, turning his attention back to the chamber as the wall clock struck 12:01 AM.

Inside the chamber, strong white-gloved hands emerged from the shadows. The executioner's grip was firm as he pulled the lever, releasing the cyanide pellets into the tank below. The deadly pellets, combined with distilled water and sulfuric acid, released a cloud of lethal gas that hissed upward from under Branch's seat.

Branch's fear was palpable. Sweat beaded on his forehead, his nostrils flared, and his chest heaved. His attempts to hold his breath were futile against the encroaching gas cloud. As the poison filled the room, Branch's body convulsed. Saliva dribbled from his mouth, and a wet stain spread across his prison uniform. The horrific spectacle was met with silence from the onlookers.

After ten excruciating minutes, a buzzer sounded, signaling the end. Branch's lifeless body slumped, his eyes rolled back, adrift in their sockets. The hissing of gas ceased, marking the end of the serial killer's life. Slowly, motors whirred into action, the venting fans working to dispel the stench of death.

The Criminal Courts Building of Los Angeles painted a different picture by day. The city's overcast sky threatened rain as life went on below. A defiant white skinhead swiped a magazine from a blind African American newsstand vendor, unnoticed in the thrum of the city. Four Crips eyed two Bloods cruising in a low-rider, a semi-automatic AR-15 threatening from the car window.

Law enforcement officers cited Asian street vendors selling hot dogs and pretzels. The wailing of police sirens wove into the city's soundtrack. The hustle of a business lunch crowd paused obediently at the "Do Not Walk" light. At the same time, a youthful rebellion was displayed by kids in Raiders jackets jaywalking without care. Homeless people shuffled around their cardboard homes on the courthouse steps, barely given a glance by the bustling passersby. Another typical day unfolded in downtown L.A.

On the courthouse steps, two federal court justices returned from their lunch break. Judge Avery L. Hennessey, a self-assured, gruff African American man of sixty, strolled alongside his younger protégé, Judge Edwin "Ned" J. Burke. The latter, an amiable family man of forty-two, bore the unmistakable signs of overwork.

Ned broke their silent communion with a query, "How did it go?"

Hennessey shrugged nonchalantly, "He inhaled it like a trooper."

"Welcome to Fascism 101," Ned retorted, his tone tinged with weary resignation.

"There's a new wind blowing, Ned, and it's about time," Hennessey asserted, scanning their surroundings.

Like hounds on a scent, the ever-vigilant paparazzi and television crews closed in on the two judges. An eager newscaster, Nancy Nikato, a pretty Asian woman in her mid-thirties, approached with her cameraman in tow, microphone extended.

"Judge Hennessey, do you think the new Fast Track law will reduce the overall level of crime in this city?" she asked, camera recording.

Hennessey paused, considering the question. "It should send a strong signal to the hardened criminal. Make him think twice before he takes another man's life."

"It sounds like the courts finally mean business," Nikato pushed, catching Hennessey as he moved past her and held the door for Ned.

Turning to Ned, she pressed, "Judge Burke, do you agree? Do you think Branch should have been sent to the gas chamber?"

Ned's face tightened. "It wasn't an easy decision, but it was the right one." He slipped past Nikato and entered the building, Hennessey following behind.

"From the Criminal Courts building in downtown Los Angeles, Nancy Nikato, Chanel Eleven News," Nikato signed off, turning to her cameraman as the doors closed behind the judges.

In the more intimate confines of Judge Burke's chambers sat Arlen Murkey, the accomplished yet parochial Attorney General.

"Still up for this?" he asked, looking up as Ned entered.

Ned sighed, dropping into his chair. "You flew all the way down here to ask me that?"

Ignoring the sarcasm, Murkey rose, pacing the room. "The

media is pretty persuasive, Ned. The ACLU says we're animals for using the gas chamber."

"What are you getting at?" Ned countered, his gaze following Murkey's movement.

"If the Ninth Circuit hadn't sat on their fat asses all these years, we wouldn't be in this mess," Murkey remarked, pausing by the window.

"You don't know that," Ned rebuked.

"I understand Judges Hennessey and Williams are dead-locked on the Graham case. I'd hate to see you waffling again, Ned," Murkey continued, turning back towards Ned.

His remark hung in the air momentarily before Ned retorted, "Did the A.G.'s office fail to file a writ?"

Murkey offered no response, his silence echoing in the room as he went to the door, a looming silhouette against the soft afternoon light that filtered into the room. He rested his hand on the doorknob, ready to exit, yet he turned back to impart one last remark.

"Nobody wanted the job, Ned." His tone was matter-of-fact, as if stating a universal truth. He paused briefly before adding, "You clean this thing up. I'll put in a good word with the Governor."

His words, hanging heavily in the air, were a potent blend of manipulation and promise, a suggestion of power and political gamesmanship. His gaze held steady on Ned for a moment longer, an unspoken challenge in his eyes before he departed, leaving Ned in the quiet solitude of his chambers.

Read Final Appeal